"Do you still like setting fires, Rand?"

As it had been so often when they were children, Julie's tone was deliberately provocative. Her motives now, however, were quite different.... And Rand's very adult response did not disappoint her.

"Fires have their uses," he murmured seductively, nuzzling the pulse that throbbed at her temple.

Arching her neck, Julie invited his lips to explore her throat, her breasts.... With each touch of his mouth he ignited tiny flames until she finally pleaded in a husky whisper, "Let's go inside and set one together."

Rand's reply was swift—and hungry. As he kissed her his hands roamed down her back and over her hips, melding her body to his. But then he broke away and said shakily, "I think we're talking inferno here."

Julie smiled and tugged him by the hand. "Uh-huh. And I don't plan on calling any firemen...."

THE AUTHOR

Jenna Lee Joyce is one of the pen names used by two friends who live eight blocks apart in Columbus, Ohio. Also known as Janet Joyce, they have collaborated on many romances, both contemporary and historical. Neither of them can conceive of a time when they'll stop working together. They say with a chuckle, "We've worn such a path between our two houses, the city may start assessing us for street improvements!"

Books by Jenna Lee Joyce

HARLEQUIN TEMPTATION
39—WINTERSFIELD
59—CROSSROADS
81—ONE ON ONE

These books may be available at your local bookseller.

Don't miss any of our special offers. Write to us at the following address for information on our newest releases.

Harlequin Reader Service
P.O. Box 52040, Phoenix, AZ 85072-2040
Canadian address: P.O. Box 2800, Postal Station A,
5170 Yonge St., Willowdale, Ont. M2N 6J3

One on One

JENNA LEE JOYCE

Harlequin Books

TORONTO • NEW YORK • LONDON
AMSTERDAM • PARIS • SYDNEY • HAMBURG
STOCKHOLM • ATHENS • TOKYO • MILAN

Published November 1985

ISBN 0-373-25181-5

1

"AND AS HIS LIPS claimed hers, Rachel knew she would never have cause to lament her destiny. Ecstasy and the excitement she craved were hers as he..."

Julie turned the page, feeling a flush of warmth as she read further. They sure knew how to write a good love scene, she thought, closing the book. A tiny smile played around the corners of her mouth as she envisioned her mother, Angela Stites, and her mother's partner Sylvia Maxwell. The romance writing collaborators, known to their public as Angel Sylver, were no doubt hard at work this very moment creating yet another novel and enjoying every minute of it.

Angela and Sylvia, both in their midfifties, were attractive, vivacious and the happiest, most well-adjusted people Julie knew. Friends since their college days, the two were closer than most sisters.

Five years ago, having grown bored with a myriad of volunteer activities, they had pooled their imaginations and talents and produced a sweeping historical novel. Their success in the literary marketplace had been nothing short of stupendous. What had started out as a lark for the two women had mushroomed into a full-time writing career.

Julie tucked the paperback under her arm and crouched to study the lower racks of books. The Honolulu bookstore carried the majority of Angel Sylver titles but the books were displayed below eye level. Gathering up all the copies of one title, she moved them to an empty rack higher up.

Her hand paused at the next title, *Destiny's Promise*, the very first Angel Sylver book. The swashbuckling tale of a female pirate and her gorgeous male captive was Julie's personal favorite, and she indulged herself, leafing through it again. "...pulse was racing as wildly and hotly..."

"That's a good book," a deep voice rumbled from far above Julie's head. "You should buy it."

Startled by the intrusion and a trifle disconcerted that the changes she had made in the display might have been observed, Julie quickly closed the paperback and tucked it under her arm along with the other Sylver book she'd selected. "I plan to," she replied evenly. She already had a well-worn autographed copy of *Destiny's Promise* on a shelf in her California apartment, but she supposed it wouldn't hurt to have two.

Seizing the chance to promote her mother's work, she expanded with a great deal of zest. "I never miss an Angel Sylver book."

"Neither do I," the man pronounced with what seemed like genuine enthusiasm. "They're the best."

Surprised and curious, Julie looked up at him. On her last visit home, her mom and Sylvia had triumphantly announced that men were making up more and more of the romance market. However, it had been Julie's experience that any man caught red-handed with a romance novel claimed to be buying the books for a wife, mother or friend—anyone but himself. The tall man standing beside her had just scored high on her test of integrity.

At least he had the courage to come out of the closet and admit his reading preference. That was something her own father wouldn't do. Professor Willard Stites, the very proper and downright stuffy head of the Denison University History Department, staunchly maintained he only read the Angel Sylver books out of loyalty to his wife, the Angel half of the pseudonym. That he read them from cover to cover in one sitting indicated to both Julie and her mother that he enjoyed them far more than he ever let on.

Staring at the man who loomed over her, Julie guessed there was probably nothing he would not admit to openly. Who would dare challenge all that muscle and sinew? His snug-fitting white pants and the striped polo shirt stretched across his well-developed torso left little of his virile form to the imagination.

From her crouched position at his feet, Julie had to look a long way up his brawny frame to see his face, but it was well worth the trouble. He had dark eyes, a strong nose and a devilish smile curved his generous mouth. His crisp brown hair lying across his forehead in delightful disarray gave him a rakish appearance that would rival that of any breathtaking hero her mother and her partner had created. In fact, he looked an awful lot like the hero portrayed on the cover of their latest work, *Destiny's Reward.*

"Ah, you read many romances?" she finally ventured, wondering what there was about this man that niggled at her memory banks. The computer in her brain kept searching through the files but failed to spit out any useful information. Perhaps she shouldn't have walked all the way from the hotel without a hat to protect her from the bright Hawaiian sun. She couldn't seem to think straight.

"Nope, just these." He bent his considerable frame beside her and casually pulled the remaining copies of *Destiny's Promise* from the lower rack and placed them at eye level. Filling his huge hands with several other editions by Angel Sylver, he straightened and quickly positioned them more prominently on the display.

Julie's brain finally found the missing file but immediately rejected the information as she stared openmouthed at the dark-haired, broad-shouldered man. *No, it couldn't be. Not here in Hawaii, for heaven's sake. That would be just too great a coincidence!* But who else would move Angel Sylver's books to a more advantageous position on the rack? She didn't think he was an employee of the bookstore or a sales rep for the publisher. He just didn't seem the type, even though she did sense an aggression in him that would certainly make him a good salesman.

If it really was Rand Maxwell, Sylvia's rascal son, he had changed dramatically. His voice was deep and rough edged, no longer a thin tenor that cracked into a high-pitched soprano at inopportune moments. He had put a lot more meat on his bones than she would ever have predicted, and it was all prime! He was easily a foot taller than when she'd last seen him, too. In those days, she'd always had to look down, not up.

How old had he been back then? Thirteen? The male of the species did a lot of growing and changing in the years that followed the entrance into puberty—all of it for the better if he was any example.

Megahunk. No other word could describe this man more accurately. Julie stared at him in undisguised admiration, this specter from her past, all grown-up and gorgeous.

The man took a step backward to view his handiwork, seemingly oblivious to Julie's intense perusal. "There, that ought to make them happy," he said more to himself than to her. Then, looking down, he returned her stare.

He studied her for a long moment, then something flickered in his eyes. His heavy brows came together slightly and his expression became thoughtful before he gave her a rakish grin. "This would, too," he announced abruptly as he reached for her.

"What…?" Julie was lifted from the floor and bent backward over his arm before she could register anything more than the one word of surprise. Her books thudded to the floor as she reached for his shoulders to keep from falling.

"Ah, my darling, come away with me," he drawled seductively. "I can't live another moment without you. It's always been our destiny to love."

Ignoring her shock, he pressed his lips to her throat, raining kisses down the smooth ivory column. "Ever since I read the latest Angel Sylver book, I've thought of nothing else but making mad, passionate love to you."

His breath tickled her skin, but it was his deep brown eyes with the golden stars around the pupils that at last brought a giggle instead of a scream. Hadn't those incredible eyes of his been the one thing about him that had always fascinated her? This crazy man could be only one person. "Skeeter?"

"I thought it was you, Stilts," he whispered against her skin. "Now let's make this look good. We've got an audience. The hero's name is Jared."

Julie swiveled her head. From her angle she could see a cluster of faces, some registering shock, others stifling laughter. It was too late to prevent a scene. They already were one.

Go along with the gag, she reasoned. Who knows? It might increase sales if word got around that the book had inspired this good-looking man to sweep a woman off her feet in the middle of a bookstore.

Wrapping her arms around Rand's square shoulders, she declared, "Jared? Oh Jared you've come for me at last. Take me away as only you can."

She closed her eyes and offered her lips. She could feel his breath against her mouth, but instead of kissing her, he began to laugh. A deep rumbling chuckle vibrated through his chest and against her breasts.

"I can't do it," he muttered softly.

"You started this, you baboon," she whispered back, grasping his head and pulling him down, forcing the kiss.

Rand stopped laughing the moment their lips met, the first touch affecting him in a way he hadn't expected. Slowly, experimentally, he covered her mouth. Surprised when she immediately opened to him and the tip of her tongue playfully tapped his, he mused that old Julie Stites had changed in more ways than just the obvious physical improvements!

Readily accepting her invitation, he swept his tongue through her mouth and fit the lush curves of her body against his. He might have gone on considerably longer if the sound of applause hadn't brought reality back to the fore. Reluctantly, he lifted his mouth from hers.

Keeping one arm firmly around Julie's slender waist, Rand delivered a sweeping bow to their tittering audience. "Only one of the many exciting scenes you'll find in the latest story from the magic pen of Angel Sylver. Better get your copy of *Destiny's Reward* while the supply lasts."

Handing out copies to the crowd, Rand sounded like a hawker in a medicine show. "Guaranteed to bring romance into your life. Be sure to give your special man his own copy. I hear these are selling like hotcakes on the mainland."

Once he'd emptied the rack of *Destiny's Reward*, he turned to Julie and whispered in her ear, "Come on, Stilts. Pick up your books and let's get out of here."

He hurried her out of the bookstore and toward the mall level of the Ala Moana Center without saying more than a few words. Julie used his silence to bring some tranquility to her racing senses. She had certainly never imagined running into Rand Maxwell in Honolulu of all places, nor being scooped into his arms and thoroughly kissed. Moreover, she would never have expected to be left so shaken by the experience.

Of course, she'd been the one to force it. Why on earth had she done that? She was definitely suffer-

ing from too much sun and had gone weak in the
head.

It had been close to fifteen years since she'd last
seen Rand. Since then, they'd both managed to suc-
cessfully elude the attempts their mothers had made
to get them together. He was how old now? Twenty-
eight?

*Of course he is, you idiot. He's only two months
older than you are and you do know your own age.*
Actually at the moment she wasn't too sure of anything, except that she was walking along hand in
hand with the best-looking man she'd seen since
she'd stepped off the plane at Honolulu airport.

But Rand couldn't really be that extraordinary
looking. Julie noted that she had better stop in one
of these shops soon and get a hat. There was no telling what other hallucinations she might suffer if she
continued to expose the top of her head to the sun's
brilliant rays.

She'd seen plenty of good-looking men on the
beach in front of her hotel—surfers and sun worshipers clad in minute scraps of material that hid
next to nothing. She'd seen mountains of bronzed
muscles since she'd arrived and the kind of male
features that rivaled Michelangelo's finest works.

Rand Maxwell had a lot more going for him than
handsome features though. She couldn't define it in
words, but he had something that was doing wild
things to her equilibrium.

He had changed a lot since he'd been sent away to
military school after his father's death. Why hadn't
she looked more closely at all those pictures her
mother had thrust in front of her nose every time
she'd gone back to Granville for a visit?

"So, what are you doing in a bookstore in Honolulu?" Rand asked, guiding her to a bench beside the Tsutakawa fountain sculpture.

"Same thing I've been doing in bookstores ever since Angel Sylver was born. How about you?"

His answer was a deep chuckle, like the one that had reverberated against her breasts earlier. The sound made her flesh tingle anew and Julie was glad she was sitting down. The sensations rushing through her would have made standing impossible.

"I'll rephrase that," he said. "What are you doing in Honolulu?"

Rand's deep-set eyes shimmered with enjoyment as he studied her, entranced by the way the Hawaiian sunlight sparkled across the thick blond waves and curls that brushed her shoulders. It was that wild mass of streaked gold and silvery ash that had first caught his attention when he'd walked into the bookstore.

That hadn't been the only thing he noticed. Julie's height, probably five feet ten or eleven, had made it difficult to miss her. But, instead of looking like the ironing board he had once labeled her, Julie had filled out in all the right places.

Who would ever have thought that the bean pole who had towered over him when they were kids would have developed breasts that made his hands ache to touch them? The soft knit top she wore was so revealing, he knew she wasn't wearing much more than the lightest wisp of a bra.

And those legs. Those incredible legs that had been the bane of his youth. Her long limbs had enabled her to best him at basketball time and time again. In fact, she had bested him at most sports. That had been humiliating and he had resented her for it.

Moreover, Julie had always been the goody two-shoes to his Peck's bad boy. Yet, when he'd guessed her identity, he'd not thought of his long-ago opinions of her, but seized his chance to kiss her wide, rosy-pink mouth—the most kissable mouth he'd seen in a long time.

Knowing she was being studied by those same brown and gold eyes that had repeatedly demoralized her in some way or another years before, Julie felt uncomfortably warm and concentrated on the cool water streaming down the sides of the sculpture, envying the colorful *koi* swimming placidly in the fountain's clear pond. "I'm combining a lot of work with a little bit of pleasure," she finally answered, wondering why she was reacting so strongly to Rand.

After all, she'd known him forever. He'd been like a pesky brother she had been forced to tolerate when they'd been children. She'd tagged him "Skeeter" because he had been small for his age, and with his constant needling was as irritating as a hungry mosquito.

Her abhorrence of him had been returned. He'd tagged her "Stilts" because of her long skinny legs that had refused to stop growing. By the sixth grade she'd soared far above him. Living in a small town and being the only children of best friends, it had been difficult to avoid each other. Much to their mothers' chagrin, they'd fought and teased each other unmercifully whenever they'd been forced to spend time together.

Always ornery and full of energy, Rand had been too much for Sylvia to handle alone after the elder Randall Maxwell had died of a cerebral hemorrhage. When the principal had threatened to expel him from junior high, and the local police department had come to know the Maxwells' telephone number by heart, Sylvia had admitted defeat for probably the first time in her life. She had enrolled Rand in a strict military school in Kentucky.

Most of Granville, Ohio, had breathed a deep sigh of relief when Rand had left, and no one more wholeheartedly than Julie. He'd been a thorn in her side and the cause of the most embarrassing moment in her life. Yet here she was in Honolulu, feeling the exact opposite of abhorrence toward her childhood nemesis—the very grown-up Randall Burch Maxwell III.

This attraction definitely had to be a side effect of the sun, the tropical atmosphere, or perhaps she was lonely. Maybe any friendly face would have brought about this strange need to throw herself into his arms. But she wasn't lonely and she knew it. She'd only just arrived in the island paradise and had a full schedule planned, one that didn't include time for socializing.

"How about you, Rand?" she asked, hoping to get him talking so she wouldn't have to arrange her words in any semblance of logical order. "Are you here on vacation?"

"Mmm?" Rand mumbled absently, lost in his study of the faint sprinkle of freckles across her nose, the rosy mouth he had so recently kissed and the thick brown lashes that framed her bluer-than-blue eyes. Those eyes rivaled the beauty of a tropical lagoon, he mused. Not really a true blue but teal. Eyes that were looking very puzzled....

"Oh...yes," he blurted, covering his momentary lapse as best he could. Trying to center his attention on their desultory conversation, he wondered, not for the first time in his adult life, why he'd been such an utterly stupid kid. "Vacation and some work."

Julie'd always had that eye color, pert, freckled nose and lush mouth. But, Rand couldn't have foretold that the rest of her would develop so well. *Ah, the ignorance and shortsightedness of youth.*

"Have you—"

"Have you—"

"Ladies first," Rand offered with another chuckle, deep dimples slashing his square jaw as the small crinkles around his eyes deepened.

Laugh lines, Julie tagged them. Funny, she'd never thought Rand laughed enough to warrant them. But then, what did she know about him now? Maybe he'd saved up all his laughter during the first thirteen years of his life, muffling it behind a forbidding glare whenever she was around.

"Have you read all the Angel Sylver books?" Julie inquired. "You seemed so knowledgeable about their latest."

"Yes I have. I guess I read the first one out of curiosity and loyalty, then got hooked," Rand admitted, shifting his position on the bench so that his arm trailed along the back just beyond Julie's shoulders. If he lifted his finger, he could twirl it right through one of her silver-gold curls. He wondered if her hair was as soft and silky as it looked.

"Me too, I mean all except their latest. Mom told me it would be out this month." Julie patted the paper sack resting on her lap. "I plan on starting it tonight."

Dumb! Now he'd know she was here alone. She inwardly flinched, expecting a taunting voice from the past to jeer at her. *Stilts, stilts. She'll sit at home until she wilts!*

Things were definitely looking up, Rand commented to himself. No evening in romantic Hawaii should ever be spent alone, but he hadn't really felt like testing his luck tracking down unattached females. That is until he'd seen Julie breezing into the bookstore ahead of him.

"*Destiny's Reward* is pretty good, maybe their best so far, but if you can tear yourself away from it, how about having dinner with me?" Rand asked. *All right, Maxwell. Here it comes.* Knowing Julie, she would choose the book over him.

"I'd like that, Rand, but I have to catch a flight out of Honolulu this evening," Julie replied vaguely. She didn't look at him, directing her attention instead to the spectacular display of flowering trees across the open mall.

"Too bad, it might have been fun," Rand responded to the negative in equally vague terms, hiding his disappointment behind a bland smile.

Julie was disappointed, too, and her expression was just as unreadable. It would have been nice to spend some time with Rand, but she had a lot of things to do before catching her flight to Maui. Realizing she'd spent far more time at the shopping center than she had planned, she took a quick look at her watch. As if on cue, Rand did the same.

Simultaneously, they rose to their feet. In a rush of embarrassed explanations, each announced an appointment elsewhere. They separated, expressing polite regret that they wouldn't be able to get together, and voicing the usual comment made by old-time acquaintances that they shouldn't let so many years go by before seeing each other again.

"MISS?" The librarian in the Bishop Museum touched Julie's shoulder. "We're closing now."

Reluctantly Julie shut the heavy volume she'd been reading. She had hoped that three hours spent in the reference library would have been enough to gather the information she had come for. The accounts of the 1868 eruptions of volcanoes on the island of Hawaii had been disappointing.

She'd known there was a strong possibility that these eyewitness descriptons would offer little new information, but there had been the off-chance that she'd run across some small new detail. Unfortunately, thoughts of Rand Maxwell had kept undermining her concentration. If there were any details that she could use here they would have to have been printed in blinking neon letters for her to notice them.

"Drat you, Skeeter," Julie mumbled aloud as she picked up her notes and other belongings. "Why didn't you beg me to change my flight?"

"Did you want something else, miss?" the librarian asked, puzzlement shadowing her lovely sloe-eyed face.

"Nothing. Pardon me. Just mumbling to myself. You know what they say about us crazy scientists," Julie offered self-consciously, more aware of her height at that moment than she had been in years. She towered over the petite young Hawaiian. Backing hurriedly through the door, she called, "Thanks again for all your help."

"Anytime," the librarian answered, shaking her head after the tall mainlander who seemed in such a hurry. Smiling to herself, she stepped into the corridor and called softly, "Remember *hoomana-wanui.*"

Julie stopped her long-legged stride and looked back over her shoulder, bewilderment narrowing her eyes. The librarian explained, smiling, "Roughly translated, it means take it easy. Don't be in such a hurry. Today is so beautiful, why reach for tomorrow?"

"Thanks. I'll keep that in mind." Julie smiled in return, appreciating the other woman's advice. One thing she'd learned almost immediately on this island was that patience and enjoyment of the moment were traits valued above all else. "And aloha."

"Aloha," the woman replied approvingly.

Hoomanawanui. That was a good idea, Julie reflected as she waited for a bus to take her back to Waikiki Beach and her hotel. This was supposed to be a vacation of sorts, the first one she'd really had in far too many years. She'd been in such a rush lately. More than just lately, she realized with a frown.

After spending her high-school years concentrating on athletics, she'd gone on to college without the slightest idea of what she wanted to do with her life. The University of Southern California had recruited her for its women's basketball team. USC and all of California was dramatically different from the

Ivy League atmosphere of Denison University in Granville, Ohio. To a seventeen-year-old Julie Stites, that and the fact that her father was a professor at Denison had been enough reason for her to accept a scholarship from an out-of-state school.

The university had done more for Julie than hone her athletic skills. It had provided her with a choice of career in a most unusual and indirect way. She'd elected to take mythology, of all things, to fulfill a humanities requirement. Her roommate had assured her it would be easy.

Mythology 101 had been designed to show how the various ancient gods and goddesses had been used by their worshipers to explain natural occurrences. At the point when rationale no longer served, supernatural forces were invoked as the ultimate causes. Julie had been particularly intrigued by the Hawaiian goddess, Pele. The deity of fire had enticed Julie into further study of volcanoes and other phenomena of the earth's interior.

Once she'd chosen a major, she raced through her courses, finishing her undergraduate work in three years and staying on for a master's degree. Upon graduating, she'd become a staff member of the privately endowed Carlton Institute in Los Angeles, which was dedicated to studying the thermal history of the earth. Presently, she was completing work for a Ph.D. in geophysics in order to become a senior member of the staff.

The Institute already recognized her knowledge and skill in the field, but she needed a doctorate to add the necessary credibility to her theories and research. Without the Ph.D. behind her name, her work would not be taken seriously around the world, nor would grants-in-aid be made available to any research bearing her name. To that goal, Julie had dedicated nearly every waking moment, with the result that her social life had become negligible.

Remembering the melodically pronounced suggestion of the librarian, *hoomanawanui*, Julie slowed her pace and strolled leisurely through the peaceful lobby of her hotel. For the first time since she'd arrived she noticed the beauty of its architecture. She was surrounded by beauty, she realized as she rode the elevator up to her room. *Why reach for tomorrow?* She didn't think she could wholeheartedly embrace that part of the island philosophy, but she could rephrase it. *Why reach back to yesterday?* Now that made a lot of sense.

It was ridiculous to let someone from her past disturb her so much that she couldn't concentrate. And that wasn't the worst part of it. Though Rand Maxwell could turn her on with one look from his marvelous eyes, he also conjured up memories from long ago that she had tried hard to put behind her.

She was no longer Julie Stites, the Stilts of Granville. She'd learned to carry her height with pride. Her body had filled out and now men turned to look at her with smiles of appreciation, not mockery. While she might not indulge in a heavy social life, she wasn't lacking in invitations.

Damn you, Skeeter. You're as much an irritant now as you were when we were growing up. She entered her room and closed the door sharply behind her. Rand Maxwell had bugged her during her childhood years and he was bugging her now.

Because of him, she'd been late getting to the Bishop Museum Research Library. Because of him, old insecurities had surfaced. Because of him, she hadn't been able to accomplish a thing today. How dare he have grown up and become so sexy!

Stripping off her clothes, she stepped under the refreshing shower. She was as exasperated with herself as she was with Rand, wondering why she hadn't gone to dinner with him. She could have left for Maui tomorrow or even the next day. Accepting her mother's invitation to take advantage of the newly purchased property meant she didn't have to worry about losing a reservation.

She was struck by a sudden suspicion. The condo was owned jointly by her mother and Rand's. Was his destination the same as hers? But her mother wouldn't do that, not when she knew Julie had come here to work.

Thinking a private villa on one of the outer islands would be the perfect place to finish her paper, Julie had borrowed one of the Institute's portable computers and headed for the islands. She needed to study volcanic activity on Hawaii firsthand and wanted to pick the brains of the staff at the Volcano Observatory. It was going to be a little inconvenient flitting back and forth from Maui to Hawaii, but unlimited free rent made up for that. Besides, Maui was a lot closer to Hawaii than California, and if necessary she could prolong her stay.

There would have been no harm in putting off her flight for one more day. If she'd had any sense, she would have asked Rand where he was staying. Then she could have called him up, explained that her flight had been changed and arranged a date.

Date? She, Julie Stites, was actually contemplating going out with Skeeter Maxwell on a real, honest-to-goodness date? She'd vowed never to do such a thing again after that long-ago disaster arranged by their mothers. Remembering that evening still brought a bright blush to her face, and Julie lowered the water temperature of the shower.

2

WHEN JULIE STEPPED OUT of the shower and began drying off, it was the image of herself at thirteen she saw in the fogged mirror. Instead of her long blond mane, she saw the short-cropped hair she'd worn back then. The practical cut had looked perfect when she'd walked out of the salon. But her waves and curls had had a mind of their own and a pre-adolescent Julie had never been able to recreate the stylish arrangement achieved by the beautician.

By the sixth grade, Julie had already reached a full five feet ten inches, but her figure development had lagged far behind her height. With her short hair, her gangly body clothed in jeans and T-shirts, she'd looked more like a boy than a girl. Even the pretty dress that had been purchased for the seventh grade spring dance, hadn't been enough to tranform her into a feminine vision of loveliness—the fantasy she'd secretly harbored beneath her tomboy surface.

"WHERE ARE YOU, fairy godmother?" Julie wailed at her vanity mirror. "I'm about to go to the ball and I still look like a stick!"

The bodice of the dotted Swiss frock definitely needed help. Quickly she started stuffing facial tissues into her bra. "There's nothing else inside this harness," she muttered as her figure started taking on more acceptable curves.

Having added as much artificial bosom as the AA cup could hold, Julie stood sideways to admire the effect. It wasn't much, but a little was better than nothing, she determined. Turning her attention to the application of lip gloss and mascara, she sighed. "Who cares, anyway? I'm stuck going to this thing with dumb old Skeeter Maxwell."

"Darling, you look so pretty," Angela Stites swept into the room and stood behind her daughter.

Julie gave her a brief glare and resumed her clumsy handling of the mascara wand. Seeing the elegantly beautiful woman standing beside her, Julie felt almost as sorry for her mother as she did for herself. There was truly no justice in life when such an exquisite creature could give birth to such a misfit. Julie decided then and there that her mother was probably the world's greatest actress if she could actually mouth compliments to her gawky daughter and sound sincere.

"Look what lovely long lashes you have," Angela complimented, taking note of, but not commenting on, the sudden fullness of her daughter's bosom.

"That's about all there is to admire," Julie grumbled, shoving the wand back in the tube of mascara. "Just hope this gunk doesn't run down my face."

"It won't, sweetheart," Angela assured, squeezing Julie's thin shoulders. "Not unless you cry, and there's no chance of that this evening."

But her mother had been wrong. The dance was one disaster after another. Arriving with Rand Maxwell had been tantamount to coming with a brother. Everyone knew their parents were close friends and that Rand had been bribed to escort Julie the few blocks to the school and to ask her for one obligatory dance. What they didn't know was that Julie had been bribed to accept. She and Rand had stumbled across the dance floor at arms's length, looking anywhere but at each other. Both of them had breathed a sigh of relief when their duty was fulfilled.

It wasn't necessary to bring a date and it didn't take long for Julie to find herself in a circle of girls only. That was okay with her, except all the girls seemed to want to talk about was how to get the boys to dance with them. Emissaries from the cluster of girls were continually being sent to the cluster of boys across the gym floor with messages as to whom was expected to ask whom to dance.

No one volunteered to be a go-between for Julie and she didn't request one. None of the boys reached much above her shoulder, and anyway, she observed, the few who ventured to ask a girl out on the floor were all pretty klutzy dancers. Why her friends actively sought that kind of foot punishment was beyond her. She was more than happy to forego dancing until the boys had caught up in height and acquired some coordination.

Julie was completely bored standing around with nothing to do. Each minute seemed like an hour. She almost shouted with joy when, finally, the band started playing the last waltz. *Fifteen more minutes*, Julie told herself, watching the clock. *Only fifteen more minutes and I can get out of here.*

"Uh, Julie...uh...um...let's dance," a breaking voice sounded next to her. Before Julie could say no, her girlfriends pushed her out onto the floor and her hand was grasped in a sweaty palm.

Her partner was Tom Hammond, the class clown and the shortest boy in the entire seventh grade. Julie knew they made an utterly ridiculous-looking pair, and by the titters coming from both sides of the gym, she realized that everyone else thought so, too. Unable to stand it, she wrenched her hand free from Tom's grasp and stomped away.

"Hey! The music's not over," Tom protested, following her.

"So what? I'm not dancing with you another minute."

"But, I'll lose five bucks," Tom admitted bluntly, trying to drag her back out on the floor.

At that, Julie whirled around and glared down at her diminutive classmate. "Someone's paying you to dance with me? Who and why?" she demanded angrily, her expression stormy enough to warrant a truthful answer.

Sheepishly, Tom revealed, "One of the guys has a camera and he wanted to take a picture of the two class freaks together for the yearbook."

"Freaks? That's what they call us?" Julie screeched, her furious face camouflaging her battered ego.

"Yeah, pretty dumb," Tom muttered as he studied the toes of his shoes. "Sorry, Julie. You're a nice girl. You really don't deserve their teasing."

His apology helped, but only to make her realize she wasn't the only one hurting. Maybe Tom covered his own feelings of inadequacy with all the clowning. "Neither do you," she mumbled as she left the gymnasium.

Rand caught up with her before she'd gotten a block from the school. By that time, the tears were flowing freely down her face. "Go away," she ordered when he came up beside her. "I don't need you. Nobody's going to jump out of the bushes and attack a freak!"

"Oh, Stilts, it's not that bad," Rand announced sympathetically and grabbed her arm to stop her. "They'll all forget it by tomorrow."

It was such a rare moment for him to champion her that Julie stopped and looked down at him with amazement. Standing up on his toes, Rand smashed his lips to hers.

Julie's bruised mouth dropped open. Never, ever had she thought her first kiss would come from Skeeter Maxwell! She was speechless and saw that he was, too. She didn't know whose face was more red.

Rand recovered far more quickly than she did, however, and Julie's discomfort increased as he started laughing. "You've got black tears all over your face." In a blink of an eye he plucked a tissue from her bodice and handed it to her. "Here."

If being called a freak hadn't been humiliation enough for one evening, Skeeter's knowledge of the contents of her bra topped it off. His laughter at her outrage didn't help, either, and she stormed home, vowing never to lay eyes on Rand Maxwell for the rest of her life.

"HOW SILLY," Julie said aloud to herself as she finished dressing for her flight. That was a long time ago and it had undoubtedly been the point in her life when her self-esteem was at its lowest. Her confidence had climbed steadily since then, and that incident had been forgotten until today.

She'd been able to face Tom Hammond and all her classmates with little trouble. But seeing Rand again brought back all those inadequate feelings. She hadn't been around him much after that dance; it was only a few weeks later that he'd been packed off to military school. Maybe if they'd had some sort of confrontation, the incident would have lost its significance and not smoldered beneath the surface as it obviously had.

Such a petty thing. Julie reminded herself, tossing items into a carryall. *Forget it. Rand probably has.* Even if he hadn't, they were both adults now and it was something they could laugh about. Then she remembered that she'd missed the opportunity to laugh with Rand about anything. The likelihood of seeing him again anytime soon was very slim.

"HELLO DEAR, or rather, aloha."

"Mom?" Julie asked, fighting a desire to hold the phone receiver at arm's length and stare at it. She'd only just walked into the Angel Sylver half of the two-unit villa when the phone had started ringing. The woman had always had an uncanny sense about Julie's whereabouts. She wondered if that was an instinct all mothers had, or if Angela Stites was exceptional.

"Did you have any trouble finding the place? I've been calling for more than an hour."

"Is anything wrong?" Julie asked anxiously. "It must be the middle of the night in Ohio."

"Everything's fine, dear," her mother assured. "I'm just calling to make sure you didn't have any problems."

"No, none," Julie replied, placated by her mother's easy tone. She hoped her smile didn't come through in her voice. She could just picture her mother pacing around the cozy kitchen in Granville for the past hour. Rarely off by more than a few minutes in her calculations of Julie's movements, the extra hour must have given Angela enough time to create a myriad of imagined disasters befalling her one and only child.

"It just took a little while to rent a car at the Kahului airport and drive across the island," Julie furnished, seeing in her mind's eye the look of relief on her mother's face. "I also stopped at a market in Maalaea. You didn't allow time for picking up groceries."

Missing the good-natured taunt, or possibly choosing to ignore it, Angela agreed, "That explains it. Well I'm glad you're there now."

"You're sure everything's okay?" Julie repeated, concern tinging her voice. "I mean, dad hasn't..."

"Your father is fine," Angela inserted quickly. "I told you not to worry about him. The doctor said it was an attack of angina, no damage, just a little warning. All he needs is a good rest."

"That's why the two of you should be over here enjoying this beautiful place," Julie advised, already aware of how peaceful and slow paced life was going to be for the next week or so.

"We're going to do that just as soon as Will feels better," Angela said. "Tell me, honey. What's the place like? I want to tell your dad all about it. We only had pictures to go on. Did we get our money's worth?"

Julie took a quick survey of her surroundings, delighted with what she saw. "I think you got a heck of a deal. I haven't seen anything except the living room and the kitchen yet, but they're both quite nice. It's almost dark so I'm not sure of the view from the front and back porches."

"Not porches, lanais," her mother corrected. "You should be able to see the bay from the front and lots of flowers and trees from the back. Tell me about the furniture and appliances."

Dutifully, Julie reported that the kitchen was well outfitted with a conventional-size range, refrigerator, microwave oven and a dishwasher. Looking beyond to the living room, she described the reed furniture, assuring her mother that the Haitian cotton cushions appeared in good condition. "It's all pretty neutral, mom. Very fresh and 'Hawaiian looking,' I guess."

She described the high ceiling, the overhead fan and the wood paneling. "Sorry I can't tell you about the bedrooms, unless you want to hang on while I go take a look."

"That's okay, dear. I have pictures of them. One is supposed to have a king-size bed and the other a double. Oh, by the way, Julie," her mother went on. "Maid service is available and I notified them that you were coming. Bed and bath linen are furnished. The beds should have been made up and everything ought to be nice and clean. You won't have anything to do but relax."

"I'll do that whenever I'm not working on my thesis."

"Now Julie," Angela began the lecture she'd delivered often in the past few years. "All work and no play is bad for the soul—"

"Don't worry," Julie interrupted, since she knew her mother's speech by heart. "I'll give my soul lots of attention while I'm here."

Sidetracked but not mollified, Angela relayed a few more details about the services provided by the condominium agency and then asked, "Is it really as romantic as it sounds? Sylvia and I have been thinking of trying a contemporary romance and using the villa as a setting."

"Probably be perfect." Julie tucked the phone under her chin and began emptying one of her two bags of groceries.

"Now all we need is a plot. Got any ideas?"

"Is that a subtle way of asking about my love life?"

"Would I do that?" Angela returned with exaggerated guile.

"You know you would." Julie opened the refrigerator, pleased to find it was clean and running, and started loading the perishables.

"It's a shame you're there all alone."

"I really do have a lot of work to do, mom. Sylvia's a better choice to do the heroine research. She's a lovely woman and shouldn't have remained a widow this long."

"Sylvia has a full social life, but I know you can't say the same thing. Some charming young man is just sitting there waiting for a lovely girl like you to come along. How's he ever going to find you if you bury yourself in work?"

"Mother, I don't have time to indulge in the great romance of the century right now, but that doesn't mean it will never happen." Julie kept her tone light, hoping to sidestep the now-familiar controversy over her single status. Her poor mother just couldn't seem to understand why none of the relationships in Julie's life had blossomed into a lifelong romance.

"Well...you never know who may turn up."

"No one should. This place isn't in the middle of a busy resort. I should think everyone would arrive paired off. Or did you have someone in mind?" Julie asked, the suspicion she'd harbored after running into Rand returning in full force.

"No, no, nothing like that," Angela negated rapidly. "Maybe the people who own the other side. Is anyone in residence right now?"

"Mmm-hmm, the owner. He said he'll be staying here for a couple of weeks. Could prove interesting." Julie purposely made her voice more provocative and her tone thoughtful. "He's very suave, tall, terribly good-looking...." She paused for a long moment, knowing her mother's romantic imagination was racing, then went on, "for someone who has thirty years on me and has been married to an absolutely delightful woman for about that long."

"Oh, you," Angela admonished affectionately. "You had me going there for a minute. Of course, with fiction I could always change that. Let's see now. He 's actually a lonely widower, not that old and—"

"Mom," Julie stopped her. "This call is costing you a fortune. You'd better work out the plot with Sylvia around the kitchen table. It'll only cost you a few pots of coffee. Better yet, you and dad get over here

and work out the story or send Sylvia over by herself. She can have the affair with the lonely
widower."

"WELL?"

"She doesn't suspect a thing," Angela answered
with a beaming smile as she hung up the phone.

"I wonder when Rand will get there," Sylvia
mused. "He was supposed to arrive tomorrow but I
called his apartment and no one was home. I'd give
anything to be a fly on the wall when he does show
up, wouldn't you?"

Will Stites shook his head, disapproval clear on
his pale features. "How could you two do this to
your own children? Have you no shame?"

"Not a bit," Angela replied. Her guileless smile
echoed by her compatriot. "All we're doing is giving them a little nudge," she rationalized. "The rest
is up to them."

"It's going to backfire," Will warned. He reached
for his pipe, muttering something about deceit and
not being a party to such goings on. "They're adults,
now, and shouldn't be victimized by such under-
handed maneuverings." Scowling when his wife
took the pipe away from him, he commented, "Fireworks. There's going to be fireworks."

"We're counting on it," Sylvia said with a giggle,
lifting her coffee cup. Angela raised hers and they
tapped the cups together in a toast.

"I'm going back to bed," Will growled, disgrun-
tled, and left the room.

THE CONDO OVERLOOKING MAALAEA BAY was
everything his mother had claimed it would be.

Rand pushed his key into the door. Having arrived after dark, it was difficult to tell exactly what the view would be like, but he could hear the sound of the ocean and assumed it could easily be seen from the lanai at the front of the one-story villa.

The single-story villas, though doubles, afforded privacy and quiet—all he really required. The steep-roofed building was one of eight arranged in a scattered sort of complex along the coast, miles away from the hustle and bustle of a large commercial resort. Its isolated location was most welcome.

It was already past midnight and Rand was fighting to keep his eyes open. Having boarded his first flight several time zones away only two days before, he still hadn't recovered from jet lag. Flipping on a light, he viewed the reed furniture and neutral decor of the living room through fatigue-glazed eyes.

It was just as well he hadn't arranged anything with Julie for this evening, he thought as he dropped his luggage. He would have fallen asleep in the middle of dinner. Yet he'd cursed himself all afternoon for not finding out where she was staying. Of course, she'd said something about catching a flight. She was probably on her way back to the mainland.

California. Wasn't that where she lived now? Maybe he'd stop there on his way home.

He was so tired, the gold-carpeted floor looked as enticing as any bed. He'd figure out a way to get in touch with Julie tomorrow. Funny, running into her like that after all these years. Sighing, he unbuttoned his shirt and pulled it out from his pants.

With no plans to keep him in Honolulu, Rand had canceled his hotel reservation and taken the last flight to Maui. It had been a long day, he acknowl-

edged, stepping out of his shoes and crossing to the
sofa. After spending hours at the East-West Center
at the university talking with various instructors,
he'd discovered that the man he most wanted to talk
with was away on vacation—on the east coast of the
mainland, no less.

They may very well have passed each other in the
air, Rand mused in self-derision, plopping down on
the sofa and swinging his feet up on the coffee table.
If he'd had any sense he would have put this trip off
a few weeks and planned it better. However, when
his mother had practically begged him to check out
her new purchase, since she was unable to do so
herself, he hadn't been able to refuse. She'd given
him a bare two days' notice before he was on a plane
from New York and skipping his way across the
country.

Strange that she had acted so helpless, Rand
thought as he leaned his head back and nestled his
shoulders more comfortably against the pillows. She
always seemed to have both feet squarely on the
ground. His mother was a very independent
woman, at least most of the time.

In students' terms, she was a pretty laid-back person. Yet she'd been absolutely frantic about his taking this trip for her, saying she couldn't get away
right then because of a book deadline or something.
He didn't understand her anxiety, but it hadn't taken
much to convince him that he could combine business with a well-earned vacation. He had the whole
summer to put together the curriculum for the course
in Asian politics he'd be teaching in the fall, and what
better place to start on it than a restful condo in the
Hawaiian Islands?

Rand yawned, staring hypnotically at the ceiling fan overhead. It did some good but it was still hot. He leaned forward, stripped off his shirt, dangling it between his knees before dropping it to the floor.

Too bad Julie had to go back to the mainland. They could have shared this place for a few days. After all, her mother owned half. Sharing a secluded hideaway in Hawaii with Julie Stites. Now that was a pleasant thought. Rand smiled to himself and nestled back into the cushions.

Yep, he should have kept his wits about him and asked her to accompany him to Maui. The stupid kid still lurked beneath the surface, he guessed. It hadn't taken Stilts long to bring him back out. He never had been able to think straight around her, much less manage intelligent speech. Today, after holding those lush curves and taking that sweet mouth, he'd regressed completely.

He was dead tired. That was another reason why he'd acted like a tongue-tied boob with Julie. . . . Maybe he'd just close his eyes for a little while and then get up and unpack before climbing into a bed for some serious sleeping.

"WHAT ARE YOU DOING HERE?" Julie demanded loudly as she none-too-gently shook Rand's bare shoulder.

Slowly opening one eye, Rand looked groggily up at her. "Be quiet, Stilts," he muttered and closed his eyes again. "Go yell at somebody else."

"Don't you dare go back to sleep, Skeeter Maxwell." She placed her hands on her hips and glowered down at his head, unconsciously reacting to him as she had when they were young. "You get up off that couch this minute!"

"Always were a nag," he grumbled, snuggling his cheek against the cushion. "Haven't changed." His steady breathing indicated he'd gone back to sleep.

Incredulous, Julie stared down at him for a full minute before she gave up and strode belligerently into the kitchen. Not caring that she was making a lot of noise, she opened and closed several cupboards in search of a coffee cup. What really galled her was not so much finding Rand asleep on the living-room sofa this morning, but knowing she'd been set up. There was no doubt whatsoever in her mind that the Angel Sylver duo was matchmaking. They were crazy if they thought she and Skeeter would make a suitable pair. He was just as irritating as ever.

It was even more irksome to realize how easily she'd walked into the trap. How could she possibly have thought running into Rand in Honolulu was merely a coincidence? Her brain had indeed not been functioning. And then that call from her mother as soon as she'd arrived...

"You never know who might turn up." Those had been her mother's very words and they should have confirmed Julie's suspicions. "Is it as romantic as it sounds?" she mimicked her mother's dulcet tones.

"It sure is," Julie grumbled as she shoved a cup of instant coffee into the microwave. Especially when the handsome hero was provided right along with the isolated hideaway. Drumming her fingers on the counter while she waited for her coffee to get hot, she nervously glanced toward the sofa at the other end of the room.

Oh, Rand was handsome all right if you liked that type. And what red-blooded woman didn't? His gorgeous chest would be perfect material for a beef-cake calendar or inspiration for a romance novel.

Julie could see the words used to describe his body as clearly as if she was curled up in her favorite chair reading them. "Curling hair covered his powerful chest muscles, arrowing downward to disappear beneath his waistband. Her gaze was drawn to his flat belly, powerful thighs straining beneath the fabric of his tight-fitting breeches. An obvious bulge…"

"Oh, stop it!" she shouted, yanking the microwave-oven door open as the timer went off.

Either her loud exclamation or the sharp shrill of the timer was enough to bring Rand off the couch. Swaying on his feet, he looked at her as if he was seeing her for the first time. "What the…" He raked his fingers through his sleep-tousled hair and stared stupefied at the petulant woman glowering back at him from the kitchen.

"What are *you* doing here?" he asked sleepily, his voice slurred.

"I already asked that one. Think up your own lines," Julie retorted, scowling as she advanced on him. "Here."

She handed him her cup of coffee. "You look like you need this more than I do. You certainly aren't too quick-witted when you wake up, are you?"

"And you're not the friendliest person in the morning, are you?" Rand growled as he sipped the coffee. "Better make another one for yourself before those wrinkles on your face become permanent."

"I'll just do that," Julie replied evenly, trying to hold on to her temper. Skeeter Maxwell had always had a knack for getting under her skin, and it appeared he still did. Not looking at him, she spooned coffee crystals into another mug and placed it in the microwave. "I assume you were in on this?" she commented, once again waiting impatiently for her morning coffee.

"In on what?" Rand pulled out one of the kitchen chairs and sat down, resting a bare ankle on his knee as he leaned back.

Rand's features were blank, his amber-accented brown eyes full of bland innocence, but Julie knew him better than that. Skeeter Maxwell had never been innocent of anything. "This setup? This put-up job?" she prompted when it appeared he had nothing more to say.

"What are you talking about?" Rand demanded in exasperation, setting his coffee down on the table with more force than necessary.

"You're just as dense as you always were," Julie deemed. Taking a sip of coffee, she finally got her first restorative dose of caffeine for the day. "You haven't changed one wit." Completely disgusted, she leaned back against the counter, as far away from Rand as possible.

He rubbed a hand across his bare chest in an absentminded manner, then yawned. "Appears to me, someone thinks its okay for us to play house."

"How astute of you. But since that's totally out of the question, when are you leaving?"

"Me? I'm not, and I'm gentlemanly enough not to demand you leave, either."

Julie groaned. "Some gentleman."

"Look, Miss Prude, I'm not the one who's bothered by the idea of sharing this place. There are two bedrooms, aren't there?"

She nodded.

Adopting a patient tone, Rand explained, "We're adults. We ought to be able to restrain ourselves."

"Restrain ourselves?" Julie exploded. "Hopping in bed with you is the furthest thing from my mind!"

"Typical prude!" Rand snorted.

"What do you mean by that?"

He crossed his arms over his chest and leaned even farther back in his chair, the same supercilious smirk on his face that Julie remembered from their childhood days. "Prudes expend a lot of energy denying that all they have on their minds is sex. For your information, I meant we should be able to restrain ourselves from killing each other. However..."

He paused and gave her bikini-clad figure a complete survey, showing open appreciation of her long, smooth legs, the flare of her hips and most especially her very exposed, full breasts. Julie felt naked but stood her ground, using all her willpower not to dash for a cover-up.

Finally, he returned his gaze to her face. His eyes glittered with mischief and he leered openly. I'm honest enough to admit that I won't turn you down if you ask me to share your bed."

"Why, you...you..." She picked up the sponge from the sink and hurled it at him. It missed, bouncing harmlessly on the carpeted floor beyond him.

"You've lost your aim, Stilts," Rand taunted, but held up his arms defensively.

"Oh no I haven't. I'm still a better pitcher than you ever dreamed of being." She reached for the next closest thing at hand. An unopened package of paper napkins flew through the air, hitting Rand squarely in the chest. He picked the package up from his lap.

"Oh yeah?" he answered her challenge. Coming up out of his chair, he held the package over his head, looking like a big-league catcher about to throw a man out on second. The napkins came hurtling back at her. Julie caught them and pitched them at his head with all the force she could muster. The soft missile was immediately caught in one of Rand's broad hands and sent back on a return flight.

The awkward missile flew back and forth repeatedly, but neither protagonist scored a direct hit. Eventually the abuse of the package took its toll, and with Julie's last throw, the cellophane split open. One hundred paper napkins exploded in the air before falling like huge snowflakes on the floor between them.

Rand and Julie stared down at the mess on the floor, then back up into each other's eyes. They broke into laughter at the same time and simultaneously dropped to their knees. "You throw a lot better than you used to," Julie complimented with a grin as she picked up a handful of napkins.

"Thank you," Rand accepted graciously. "You've improved, too," he complimented, but the flattery was not for her pitching skill.

In companionable silence, they duck-waddled their way to the middle of the kitchen floor, picking up napkins as they went. Knees touching, they stopped, each clutching a soft pile of flower-strewn paper. Even though they were startled by the unexpected contact, neither moved away.

Taking advantage of their proximity, Julie studied Rand's face. She liked the way his sleep-tousled hair fell jauntily across his forehead. His jawline showed the shadow of a night's growth of beard, giving his features an even more rakish appearance. Julie was struck again by his resemblance to the latest Angel Sylver hero.

"As you said, we're both adults now," Julie remarked with a nervous giggle. Picturing the scene just past in her mind's eye, she suggested, "Maybe we should start acting like it."

"I believe we can manage," Rand returned with a husky edge to his voice as he handed her his share of the paper collection. His gaze dropped to her breasts, which spilled generously beyond the edges of the blue triangles held precariously in place by narrow ties. "You sure don't need Kleenex anymore."

Julie groaned, flushing scarlet from head to toe. Not wanting him to see how much the reminder had bothered her, she sprang to her feet and hurried across the small kitchen. Keeping her back to Rand, she shoved the napkins in an empty drawer and stared out the sliding glass door at the back of the room.

Rand came up behind her. Placing his hands on her waist, he gently turned her around to face him. Not quite able to hide the twinkle of laughter in his eyes, he nevertheless apologized. "Sorry I brought that up, Julie. I didn't mean to embarrass you. I figured you could laugh about it now."

"It was pretty funny, wasn't it?" She laughed somewhat distractedly, more concerned with her reaction to the touch of his palms resting lightly on her hips than the reminder of that long-ago encoun-

ter. She kept her eyes glued to his Adam's apple.
That seemed the safest place to look.

If she dropped her gaze at all, she didn't think she'd
be able to control her breathing, for she'd be confronted with the sight of a brawny, hairy chest a
scant inch away from the tips of her breasts. The
thought of how her near-naked bosom would feel
pressed up against that solid wall of masculine muscle made her nipples grow taut.

If she looked up, she'd be confronted by his wide
sensual mouth, and she already knew how it felt
pressed to her lips. She also knew how she responded to his kisses. If prudes had nothing but sex
on their minds, then she was definitely one of them.

"Funnier to me than to you at the time," Rand
said. "Even if I did pull that stunt because I felt like
such an idiot for kissing you. It was a thoughtless
thing to do. As thoughtless as that clumsy kiss," he
added, knowing the last statement was a lie.

Even after all these years he could still remember
exactly why he had kissed her that night—he'd realized for the first time that she was beautiful, and
he'd wanted to discover if her mouth was as soft and
smooth as it looked. With little courage and no fi-
nesse, he was lucky to have avoided splitting her lip.

"Until you reached for a Kleenex, I thought you
were being nice," Julie recalled, mesmerized by the
golden shimmer in his dark eyes.

"My thoughts about you could never be described by such a bland term as 'nice,'" Rand said
softly, pushing her chin up with one finger. "But I
sincerely apologize to the very sensitive young girl
inside the beautiful woman for the thoughtlessness
of the totally insensitive young twirp I used to be."

He looked deep into her eyes and Julie gained a small insight into the mature man Rand had become. "The sensitive young girl accepts the apology," she said quietly.

"And the beautiful woman?" The broad hand at her waist slid around to her back, pushing her against him. "Does she forgive the man?" he asked as he brought his face closer to hers.

"She doesn't know the handsome man well enough to know," Julie breathed, conscious of every inch of her flesh where it touched his.

"Then she'll just have to get to know him better, won't she?" he murmured huskily against her lips.

"Mmm, maybe she should," Julie whispered, sliding her palms up his chest to curl at the base of his throat.

3

RAND BRUSHED HIS LIPS softly over Julie's. At first the kiss was gentle, full of inquisitive warmth, but it became hotter and more insistent, and he gathered her closer. His hands roamed over the bare skin of her back, then settled possessively against the small of her back.

Ignoring all the reasons why she shouldn't be letting this happen, Julie rose on her toes. Wrapping her arms around his shoulders, she buried her fingers in the wavy hair at his nape. Nothing seemed to matter but the pleasurable feeling of his sensual mouth over hers, of being encircled in his arms, fitting snugly against his solid body.

His tongue teased the corners of her mouth, courting then retreating, until she emitted a soft entreaty for more. Eagerly, he took what she offered, his tongue initiating a gentle exploration of her mouth.

"You're delicious," he murmured against her moist lips. "Your turn. Kiss me, Julie. Start to know me."

She followed his thickly growled order just as eagerly as he had accepted her invitation. All her senses were attuned to the investigation, learning the secrets within the warm cavern of his mouth while her fingers discovered the texture of his chestnut hair.

It was thick, soft but not silky, springy but not wiry. She inhaled his scent, detecting faint traces of a woodsy cologne, coffee and something more—a manly essence that was uniquely his.

Running his hands down the flawless skin of her back and up again, molding her against him, Rand recalled how many times his boyish fantasies had been about Julie. About the time he'd gone off to military school, his hormones had become active, and his thoughts had turned toward the opposite sex, centering on the only girl he'd known very well. He had often dreamed about touching her like this. Even at thirteen, she had seemed like a blond goddess and far above him. He was, after all, a mere mortal. Her sublime blue eyes had shone with superior intelligence, her natural grace had given her the coordination to do all things well. Whenever he'd been around her, he'd stumbled over two left feet and had been forced to say outrageous things in order to save face. How she would have laughed had she known how he dreamed about her!

Rand's heart began to pound. Julie wasn't laughing at him now. She was kissing him back! He was holding her, touching her, and she wasn't pulling away.

Julie could feel the strong beating of Rand's heart against her breast. It was no longer a case of imagining the touch of his chest against hers; the reality was a far more potent stimulant than the fantasy. When Julie found herself being pulled gently but firmly between his thighs, she went willingly, seeking the greater intimacy.

Except for three very fragile scraps of fabric, she was naked in his arms, her flesh so highly sensitized it registered every plane and ridge of his virile body. She measured the breadth of his shoulders, the thickness of the heavy deltoid muscles that padded the juncture of his shoulders. But like an irresistible magnet it was the muscled column of his neck and the springy hair at his nape that called her hands back.

The faint rasp of his chest hair, the rough texture of his pants scraping against her sensitive thighs, made her tingle in growing excitement. A liquid warmth began low in her belly, spreading in an ever-widening eddy of pleasure, tinged with frustration, when he arched his hard groin against her.

His palms ran lightly down her spine, cupped her buttocks, then slid back up her sides. His thumbs brushed the outer curves of her breasts, edging beneath the triangular covering. "Hello, beautiful lady," he said against her cheek, nibbling a line toward her ear.

Julie lowered her heels back to the floor and rested her forehead on his shoulder. "Oh, Rand, this is crazy," she protested weakly against his skin, unable to stop herself from running her lips along his collarbone and then up his throat. She found the bristled texture of his beard exciting, further testimony that he was a man and no longer the smooth-skinned boy she had despised.

"Why crazy?" He tugged gently at her earlobe with his teeth, then directed his attentions to her neck, trailing his lips downward, across her shoulder and back again.

A shiver trickled down Julie's spine as his hot breath teased the sensitive spot at the base of her neck. "This can't mean anything," she murmured, stringing kisses along his upper chest.

"Why not?" He continued his own foray up her throat, along her jaw and back to her ear.

"We've always hated each other, that's why."

Some kind of reason returned as soon as the words were out of her mouth. Julie dragged her hands away from his shoulders and trailed them down his chest. Pushing gently, she created an inch or two of space between them.

With a deep sigh, Rand pulled her back against him, held her tightly for a long moment, then released her. "We were kids then, Julie," he reminded, his breathing not yet under control. "I wouldn't call how we're acting childlike, and as for the dislike, I'd say we've outgrown that attitude toward each other, wouldn't you?"

There was a stillness in his body, as if her answer meant everything to him. But she knew that couldn't possibly be the case. Her opinion of him had never mattered before. "Have we?"

"I like your mouth," he decreed, annoyed at her answer. "I like the feel of your skin, the softness of your breasts. I've discovered quite a bit to like about you, and I'm guessing you've reached a similar conclusion."

"Yes, well...physically..." Julie trailed off and sidestepped him. She moved on shaking legs to the table and sank into one of the chairs. Never in her life had she reacted so immediately and powerfully to a man. Why did it have to be Skeeter Maxwell? "We still don't know much about each other."

Rand leaned against the cabinets, his arms spread wide and his hands gripping the edge of the counter behind him. "We've known each other since we were born. I remember when you lost your two front teeth and when you first learned how to ride a bicycle, and I'm sure you can recall the same things about me," he said, exasperation coloring his tone. "Just what *is* bothering you, Julie?" His glorious eyes searched her face, reaching into her and demanding an honest answer.

Julie gestured with a sweeping motion of one arm, "All of this."

He stared at her, raising a quizzical brow. "So we were set up. What's the big deal?"

"I don't like being manipulated. Do you?"

Heaving himself away from the counter, Rand crossed to her, picked up his mug and deliberately evaded her question. "I'd like another cup of coffee. How about you?"

Though Julie knew the last thing she needed was a stimulant, she nodded her agreement. Rand picked up her mug and repeated the task she had performed earlier. Julie noticed with some satisfaction that his hands weren't too steady. She knew hers wouldn't have been, either. In fact, every limb of her body was still quivering.

Rand stood before the microwave, watching the lighted window as if it were a television screen. Julie used the time to compose herself, employing every kind of control she knew to bring her erratic breathing back to normal. Gradually one cause of her accelerated vital signs was replaced with another. Anger was just as effective in raising one's pulse rate as desire.

The knowledge that she and Rand were probably reacting exactly as their mothers had hoped made her furious. She'd always hated being maneuvered into something even if, given time, she might have initiated the activity herself. Perversely she would deny wanting or enjoying whatever it was until the bitter end. It was a negative trait she'd recognized in herself during her teenage years—one that, as an adult, she had tried to keep under control. She'd done a pretty good job of it in recent years, but the situation she now found herself in brought out the worst in her.

She flatly refused to have her love life arranged for her. That Rand seemed so ready to accept the situation fueled her ill temper. The one thing she'd been able to count on about him when they'd been children had been his resistance to their parents' attempts to push them together. Given past history, he should be as furious as she.

By the time Rand placed two steaming mugs of coffee on the table and sat down across from her, Julie was ready to explode. Unable to help herself, she asked belligerently, "Doesn't the fact that we've been set up bother you at all?"

"Not as much as it bothers you," he responded calmly.

Julie did not reply. She needed time to formulate her thoughts before revealing how strongly she felt about this put-up job.

Holding the gaily painted mug between his large hands, Rand studied her over the bright yellow rim, taking in her stormy features, especially the chilling fury flashing in her blue-green eyes. Her chin was set in the stubborn line he remembered so well. It might have been years since he'd last seen her, but he recognized that expression and knew what was coming unless he found a way to redirect her energies, distract her from her view.

He'd have to handle her very carefully. He didn't want to lose her now that he'd finally found the guts to reach out and take what he wanted from her. Nothing was going to prevent him from doing it, not even her. Her response had far exceeded his expectations, and he vowed it wouldn't be the last time he'd experience such flaming pleasure. It wouldn't be hard to stoke those embers to life once more, but if he made a mistake that fire could work against him rather than for him.

She had probably expected him to condemn this arrangement. However, for him their being together this way seemed like a long-awaited dream come true. Besides, he was having trouble concentrating on anything but that gorgeous body of hers. No matter how hard he tried, his eyes repeatedly drifted to her beautifully formed breasts and his body ached with the memory of how perfectly she'd fit against him. It took all of his willpower to stay on his side of the table.

And he thought he had learned to temper the impetuous side of his nature! He'd have to go at this a little more slowly—probably a lot more slowly, given Julie's basic personality. If ever a situation called for a cool head it was this one, but it was going to be damn hard. The rewards would be well worth it, but he didn't know if he could muster that much patience.

Rand swallowed several times and his voice had a strained quality when he finally spoke. "I can see you won't be content until we've had a serious discussion and worked out a set of rules or procedures. You were always good at that sort of thing," he threw in wryly and received a furious glare in response.

With an abrupt change of subject he continued, "I don't know about you, but I'm starving. At the risk of sounding like a male chauvinist, I'd appreciate it if you'd fix some breakfast while I take a shower and shave."

He grinned at her sputtered negative, the grooved dimples in his cheeks deepening. "I promise I won't expect that every morning."

He pushed away from the table, picked up one of his bags and started in the direction of the bedrooms. "Which one will you give me permission to use?"

"Have you granted me squatter's rights or something?" Julie asked, wondering why he had to be so blasted good looking. Where was she when God passed out such incredible dimples? Two months too late, she jokingly answered herself.

"Seems fair. You were here first," he conceded congenially, his eyes taking on their familiar twinkle when he saw humor sparkle in hers.

"You've got the smaller one down the hall. The bathroom's in between." She scooted her chair back and carried their mugs to the sink.

Rand hoisted another bag over his shoulder and headed toward his assigned room. Just before he turned down the short hallway that separated the bedrooms from the living area, he glanced back over his shoulder. "Uh, Julie?"

"Yes?" She turned around to face him.

"Do me a favor and put something on over that bikini."

He started to step around the corner, but Julie's quick retort stopped him. "That works both ways, Rand. Put on a shirt!".

"See, it's started," he returned cryptically. In response to her quizzical expression, he explained, "We're getting to know each other as adults, and we already know one new thing. Our bodies are driving each other crazy."

"THIS PINEAPPLE is like nothing I've ever eaten," Rand remarked, popping the last of a dripping chunk into his mouth and licking the juice from his fingers.

Julie's tongue caught the juice streaming down her arm before she agreed. "It was picked right out of the field yesterday. After this we'll be so spoiled we'll never eat a pineapple that isn't ripened by the sun."

She dangled her sticky fingers over her plate. "I don't know about you, but I could use a bath. That's the messiest breakfast I've ever had."

"I can think of better ways to get the juice off than a bath," Rand teased, reaching across the table and trailing a finger down her damp chin.

She swatted his hand away. "Skeeter. . ." she warned.

Grinning, pure mischief dancing in his eyes, he got to his feet and strode toward the door. "If you're going to be so stuffy about it, Stilts, there's a beautiful bay out there. Let's go for a swim, instead." He paused on the threshold and added, "Last one in has to do the dishes when we get back."

"No fair!" Julie sprang to her feet. "We need towels and lotion and I'm barefoot," she wailed, but

Rand was already out the door. "Come back here, you old Skeeter the Cheater!"

"You called?" he inquired solicitously, sauntering back into the villa with an air of boyish innocence.

"Yes, I did. You're taking unfair advantage," she declared as she strode toward him with a stubborn set to her chin. "I fixed breakfast, and I'm not going to get stuck with the dishes because you started a race before I was ready. We're going to do this fair and square or you'll be up to your elbows in dishwater."

"You always have to lay down the rules, don't you?" he taunted with a maddening smirk. "But it's okay. I don't plan to lose."

Julie advanced on him, grabbed a handful of his sweatshirt and dragged him farther into the room. "You wait right here until I get everything we need and some shoes on my feet. If the path down to the beach is like the front walkway, it's strewn with rocks and crushed shells. I'm not racing after you on an unfamiliar course without some protection." Eyeing his bare feet, she instructed, "You'd better put some shoes on, too."

Amusement glimmered in his eyes and the edges of his mouth turned up slightly. "Like I said, you always were a nag—and much too cautious."

"It's for your own good and you know it," Julie chided as she scurried around gathering up supplies. "The Hawaiian sun is a lot stronger than people think," she instructed as she plopped the wide-brimmed straw hat she'd picked up at the market on her head. "You're darker than I am, but even your skin won't be able to take much of it without some protection."

"Yes, ma'am," Rand got out between chuckles as he slipped his feet into the pair of canvas loafers he'd left in the middle of the floor the night before.

"What's so funny?" she demanded, reappearing from her bedroom laden down with towels, a beach bag and a blanket.

He relieved her of the blanket and flipped the brim of her hat with his middle finger. "You are. One minute you're the most seductive woman I've ever seen, even if you have tried to cover up all those curves under this shapeless flowered thing you're wearing. The next, you're running around here shouting orders and giving lectures like a harried mother. You're not the same girl I knew, that's for sure. As I recall, the last time we played house, you wanted to be the dad."

Julie ignored the part about being seductive and the part about playing house. "This shapeless thing is a muumuu. At least I've made some concessions to native custom. That ratty old sweatshirt you've got on would be better suited for the basketball court than the beach."

"If I went native," Rand warned, a sensual glint in his eyes, "you'd be even more upset."

"Humph," Julie choked out, forcing back the sudden picture she had of Rand in a flowered loincloth—or less. "Well, one of us needs to think about the consequences of being under the hot tropical sun, and that somebody certainly isn't you. You're as rash as you ever were and still something of a bully."

Besides steering the conversation in a safer direction, she intended her remark to remind him of what hadn't been said. They had never gotten around to the discussion she had planned for breakfast and she hoped her double entendre would prompt him to bring it up. She wanted to know the rules of this game up front.

Rand either chose to ignore her reminder or missed the opening she had provided. After slinging the blanket over his shoulder, he scooped up a pipe and a leather tobacco pouch and handed them to her. "Got room in your bag for these?"

"You smoke a pipe?" That explained the faint tinge of tobacco in his taste and scent, but a conservative pipe didn't fit with the devil-may-care image she had of him.

"Yep, its my only vice," he announced, open amusement dancing in his eyes and around the corners of his mouth at her disbelieving expression.

Not waiting for her assent, he dropped pipe and pouch into her bag. "If you're ready, I am." He pulled open the door and gallantly swept his arm toward the outside. "After you, madam."

"No race?" Julie inquired with suspicion, stepping through the door and quickly down the wooden steps. As soon as her feet were on the pebbled path that led to the beach, she shifted her bundles and geared her body for a quick takeoff.

"Nope." His negative was so unexpected, Julie's suspicion increased. He came up beside her, placed his arm around her shoulders and matched his longer stride to hers.

"Don't look so worried," he chided playfully. "I'm not going to shout 'ready, set, go' when you least expect it. I've decided to exercise some caution. You're right. One should be familiar with the racecourse before setting out on it."

"Glad you agree," she grumbled.

The path's grade sharpened as it wound down the cliff, adding credence to Julie's caution. However, it was as beautiful as it was treacherous and Julie's mood lightened considerably. *Hoomanawanui.* What a wonderful attitude, she thought, remembering the librarian's advice. It was a philosophy that kept the blood pressure down and was probably the best medicine in the world to prevent ulcers.

Surrounded by nature's splendor, why worry about anything but the beauty of the day? Serious or negative thoughts could wait for another time. The path was bordered by flowering trees, shrubs and vines. The air was filled with the scent of the ocean and the perfume of the blossoms: plumeria, jacaranda, ginger, hibiscus and bougainvillea. She wasn't at all positive that she was identifying the plants properly, but it didn't matter.

At last the jagged shore appeared before them. Clearly visible farther up the coast was Maalaea's small harbor. Gaily colored boats bobbed up and down in the quiet water, sheltered from the larger swells of the open sea that surged farther out. Fishermen in traditional outriggers were already returning with their morning's catch.

Beyond the harbor was a breathtaking view of the west Maui mountains, tinged lightly with pink from the morning sun and topped by fluffy clouds. Fine white sand formed a beach with large rocks scattered here and there tossed by the mighty hand of the Pacific. No other humans had yet arrived to mar the magic or serenity of the tiny cove.

"Beautiful," Julie breathed, dropping her bundles to the sand and swiftly stepping out of her shoes.

"Ready, set, go," Rand shouted from behind her.

"You rat!"

Julie didn't waste any more energy shouting. Her long legs began an instant sprint across the beach. She pulled the colorful red muumuu over her head as she ran, throwing it behind her as she entered the foaming water. Knees high, she bounded through the shallows, but Rand was still yards ahead of her. The grin of triumph he threw back at her was the last thing she saw before his head disappeared into the curl of a wave.

Not wanting to be caught beneath the crest, Julie dove headfirst into the shoulder of the wave. Using all the expertise she'd gained while living in California, she dug into the coiling water and burrowed through to the other side. She broke the surface to discover Rand waiting for her, treading water a few feet away.

"The dishes are yours," he announced jubilantly.

Julie smacked the surface of the water in protest. "I never agreed to the stakes."

"Aha! A poor loser." His long arms cut through the water and brought him alongside her.

"Come on, Julie," he begged, sounding much like the little boy he'd once been. "Give me my small victory. It's probably the first one I've ever had over you."

"Was that what this was all about?"

"Darn right," he admitted, his eyes bright with exultation.

Realization that the race might have been an unconscious example of Rand's competitive attitude toward her gave Julie quite a jolt. What other kind of goals had he set for himself where she was concerned? What other victories did he hope to attain?

Maybe his exciting lovemaking, that reduced her to a quivering mass of sensation, was just another way of showing her that he could finally best her. That would explain why he wasn't bothered by the obvious maneuverings of their parents. Perhaps her being at the condo hadn't come as a surprise to him at all.

With long smooth strokes, she set out on a course parallel to the shore, aware that Rand was following and surprised that he wasn't trying to race with her or even catch up. She was thankful for whatever reason kept him some distance behind for she wasn't ready to face him until she'd thought the situation through. If they stayed at the condo together, she knew it was probably just a matter of time before she succumbed to the longings he aroused in her. What she didn't know was whether she wanted that to happen.

Julie forced herself to set an easy, relaxed rhythm as she moved through the water. The warm waves had washed away the sticky remains of her breakfast, and the demanding surf was beginning to drain the sexual tension from her body. Though the heated attraction between herself and Rand had cooled somewhat once they'd plunged into the water, she had still felt an underlying current. Being anywhere near him was like being hooked up to a high-voltage battery.

She flipped over on her back and floated, closing her eyes against the brilliant overhead sun. Thinking about the childhood she'd been forced to share with Rand, she remembered that competition had been the main element of their relationship once they'd graduated from the sandbox. It was always who could run the fastest, throw a ball the farthest, jump the highest makeshift hurdle.

Once, they'd actually held their own Olympics in the Stites's backyard, inspired by the real games being played in far-off Mexico that same summer. Nature not being fair to the sexes in rates of growth and maturity, Julie had had the advantage of several inches of height and far better coordination. The win-loss columns had been heavily weighted in Julie's favor, and Rand had not taken his defeat well. Nor, looking back on it, had Julie been a particularly gracious winner.

Recalling her self-important boasting and Rand's vow to get her someday brought Julie immediately back to the present. It was ridiculous to think he might still be carrying such a childish grudge, but what did she really know about the grown-up Rand Maxwell? A potent chemistry was certainly working between them, but then it had always been like that. During those early years, they'd set sparks off on each other. Now, however, those sparks could well lead to something far different than a mud pie in the face. Something far more damaging.

Dropping her feet toward the bottom and treading water, Julie looked around her, surprised to discover she was alone. Gazing toward land, she saw Rand watching her from the shore. His vigilant demeanor was apparent to Julie even from the distance that separated them. It was then that she realized just how far out she'd swam.

Taking advantage of the swells moving toward the coastline, Julie let the water do most of the work. It wasn't until she was nearing the line of breakers that she had to struggle hard against the rip to keep from being swept back out to sea. Her strength was waning when she swam up the scend of the final wave, went over the crest and landed in the trough. The wave broke over her head and she was helpless to do anything but curl into a ball and go with the movement of the water until she could fight her way back to the surface.

Saving her energy for the battle to come, she concentrated on conserving air when a heavy clamp encircled her waist. She fought against it until her head was above the surface and she realized Rand had pulled her out. Without a word, he dragged her toward the shore, finally dropping her like a wet rag onto the blanket.

"I didn't need any help!" she asserted between spasms of coughing.

"Sure you didn't," Rand said sarcastically as he smacked her firmly between the shoulder blades. "Just what were you trying to prove by swimming out that far and staying out there so long?"

"I wasn't trying to prove anything and I wasn't out there all that long."

"I've been sitting up here on the beach watching you for close to half an hour." He dropped down beside her, an arm thrown over his eyes to shield them from the sun.

Sufficiently recovered, Julie rolled onto her back and bit out angrily, "If you were so worried about my being out there, why didn't you stay beside me? Then you could have proved how superior you are by dragging me in when you'd decided I'd had enough?"

Rand didn't answer at first. Eventually he levered onto his side, propped his upper torso up on one elbow and loomed over her. "Some gratitude for saving your life. I suppose you'd be happier if I'd just let the current carry you back out to sea. You're so damned stubborn, you would have floated all the way over to China before admitting that somebody else might know what's good for you. That's why I didn't try to signal you to come in. Knowing you, you would have stayed out there on purpose just to prove that no one can tell you what to do."

Irked by the realization that he knew her too well, Julie defended herself. "That's not true. I'm not stupid!"

Rand raised one brow but didn't say the words Julie expected. Instead he relaxed slightly, rearranged his long-limbed body until he was cupping his head with one hand. In a more reasonable tone, he continued, "Let's get this straight before we digress into a full-fledged battle. For starters, I left you alone because you seemed to want it that way. I didn't see any sense in forcing my company on you when you obviously didn't want it. I swam around out there for a while and then came in and waited for you.

"I was just about ready to damn the consequences and come out after you when you finally started back. Then you got caught up in that wave, and I acted on pure instinct. I'm sure you'll correct me if I'm wrong, but it certainly looked as if you were in trouble."

Julie, who had been staring petulantly out at the ocean, stole a quick glance at Rand once he'd finished. The anger was gone and his features had softened perceptibly. He was waiting for her to say something and she felt she owed him some kind of an apology. "You were right, I was in trouble. Thanks, Rand."

"That's better," he remarked softly, an irresistible smile spreading across his face. He tapped her nose with the tip of his finger then trailed it down to her lips. Pushing at the corner of her mouth to turn it up, he forced the smile she was trying to hide.

He leaned closer, moved his hand to her shoulder and turned her body toward his. "Come over here, Miss Perversity."

NO. DON'T DO IT, Julie warned silently, willing herself to resist the gentle tugging of Rand's hand. She tried to ignore the soft request in his eyes, ignore the pull of the bright amber that glimmered amid the rich chocolate of his irises. Her body ignored her mind.

Like steel filings drawn to a magnet, she rolled toward him. As his hand skimmed down her back, warming her skin and inflaming her senses, she moved closer. On some tenuous conscious level, Julie rationalized that being held in his arms was such a pleasant experience, she'd be a fool not to indulge in it again, if only for a little while.

Kissing and being kissed in return was an enjoyable pastime she hadn't indulged in for a very long time. Why deny herself any longer? She could keep things under control. As thrilling as Rand's caresses were, she could stop them whenever she chose. For now, for just a few moments, she chose not to.

Don't jump on her, Rand warned himself, willing his body to remain relaxed. He could read the play of thoughts reflected in her eyes as easily as if they were words floating across the teal depths: hesitation, wariness. She'd always been cautious, always thinking. Yet there was hunger, too.

Don't think, Julie. For once just let it happen, he entreated silently while he commanded himself to exercise restraint.

At the first contact, Julie was sure the saltwater that still beaded their flesh sizzled and evaporated. She burned wherever her skin came into contact with his, but instead of pulling back, she leaned closer. When Rand's mouth covered hers, she was eager, impatient, for the invasion of his tongue. Salt from the ocean mingled with his taste, seasoning the flavor that was Rand and whetting her appetite for more.

Her hands splayed across his back, exploring the heavy muscles that rippled and bunched beneath her touch. She strained her body to his, felt his heart beating against her breast, his taut, hair-grazed belly flat against her smooth one. Barely encumbered by brief swim trunks, his hardened virility pressed against her hipbone and Julie unconsciously shifted to cradle him with feminine softness.

"Julie...." Rand's husky pronouncement of her name called out to her before he rolled atop her and took her mouth again.

Julie answered by bending her knees and straining upward. Her arms came around his broad back to hold him tight, then her hands swept down to his flanks, her palms and fingertips recording every taut line, every corded muscle that she encountered. Never still, Rand's hands roamed over her. Everywhere he touched, he elicited a magic of response until Julie's entire being was suffused with the sensual ache that had begun deep within her.

Hesitation, caution, all thoughts fled when Rand slipped her bikini top away from her body and covered her breasts with his hands. Releasing her mouth, he moved his lips down her throat and across the swell of voluptuous bounty he treasured in his palms. Only two meager garments prevented complete intimacy, and as Rand's mouth took possession of her nipple, Julie's fingers moved beneath the stretch fabric of his trunks toward their objective.

Rand groaned his pleasure against her breast, then abruptly froze. Raising his head he looked toward the path that led back up the cliff. He swore vehemently. "We're about to have company."

Julie stared wide-eyed into Rand's anguished features. The voices floating through the vegetation at the edge of the beach had the same effect as a cold wave crashing over their heated bodies. Shock instantly replaced desire.

In a flurry of frenzied movement, they scrambled apart. Julie lunged for her top, slipped it on and fumbled with the ties at her back while Rand rearranged his trunks.

"Let me, you'll never get it," Rand ordered in a low uneven voice. He brushed Julie's shaking fingers aside and fastened the strings together.

The thin blue fabric of Rand's trunks did little to hide his arousal and he rolled onto his stomach, a pained expression on his face. Rand and Julie exchanged inspecting looks and assured each other with a nod that they were presentable just as a middle-aged couple stepped onto the sand.

"Just stretch out and act natural," Rand suggested, attempting to follow his own advice.

"Hello, Julie," hailed a silver-haired woman wearing a flamboyant muumuu and gaily decorated straw hat.

She carried a large canvas bag. Her cheerful greeting was echoed by her companion who was wearing a matching flowered shirt but a plain hat. He carried a wicker basket and a beach umbrella. It was clear the couple wasn't just out for a stroll but intended to spend some time on the beach. The Eden that Julie and Rand had enjoyed with such abandon, was being invaded. Suddenly all that had seemed so right, so very perfect and natural, was ruined.

Julie groaned softly as she recognized the intruders. She raised her hand in a weak salutation, and whispered under her breath, "It's the Sellinghams. They own the other half of the villa." Rand's answer was a long-suffering roll of his eyes.

The elderly couple covered the stretch of white sand in what Julie was sure was record time, coming to a halt a few feet away from where she and Rand lay posed in what they hoped were casual positions. Julie's breath was still uneven and she was sure every one of her seventy inches was beet red with embarrassment. Getting slowly to her feet, she forced a smile.

"Mrs. Sellingham. Mr. Sellingham. How good to see you this morning," she lied.

"Lovely morning for a swim," Candace Sellingham commented, her eyes straying to Rand then back to Julie. "This is such a beautiful beach, but then the whole island is just breathtaking."

"Yes. Yes, it is," Julie agreed.

The island was less breathtaking, however, than the moments she'd just spent in Rand's arms. She'd been so spellbound by his kisses and caresses, she'd been blind and deaf to anything else, hadn't seen the beauty of her surroundings or heard the warnings of her conscience. Thank heaven, Rand had noticed the Sellinghams' approach when he did or the couple would have had more than the scenery to feast their eyes on.

A few comments were exchanged about the beach, the ocean, the sky. All the while, the Sellinghams were eyeing Rand intently. When Julie had met them the evening before, she'd made no mention of a husband or friend staying with her. She'd heard that it was very easy for an unattached female in Hawaii to find male companionship on the beaches. What if they thought Rand was a local beach bum she'd picked up?

"I'd like you to meet Rand Maxwell. He's my...He and I are..." Julie gulped and paused, not knowing how to explain Rand's presence to the Sellinghams without offending their moral sensibilities.

"You'll have to forgive Julie," Rand supplied with a wide grin as he jumped to his feet. Keeping a concealing towel draped over one arm, he offered his free hand to Gene Sellingham. "We just got married and she's not used to her new status yet. I understand you and Mrs. Sellingham are our neighbors."

"You're newlyweds?" Candace Sellingham's considering expression was quickly replaced by a beaming smile. "We should have known. Gene and I were just saying what a shame it was that Julie was staying here all alone."

"I couldn't join her until late last night," Rand put in smoothly. "We're on our honeymoon, but we both have a few business obligations to take care of on Oahu while we're here in the islands."

With perfect ease, he elaborated on the lie. "Thought we could write some of this trip off if we combined a bit of business with pleasure. On my salary, every little bit helps."

"Rand!" Julie couldn't believe he'd actually say such outrageous things, but if she denied them, she could just imagine what the Sellinghams would think.

Rand wrapped an arm around her shoulders and gazed down at her with loving eyes. "She hates it when I talk about our honeymoon like that. Thinks it takes away from the romance."

His eyes said that nothing could do that and even knowing he was putting on an act, Julie blushed beneath his heated stare. Her mumbled protest came across as the endearing reaction of a bride whose new husband openly reveals his overwhelming desire to have her all to himself. She could have died when the Sellinghams quickly apologized for having intruded upon their privacy.

"Nonsense," Rand negated, charm oozing from every pore. "Actually, we were just about to go back up to the villa, weren't we, darling?"

"Mmm." Julie nodded, amazed even that much could get past her clenched teeth.

Gene asked them how long they were staying, then extended an invitation to come over to their place for drinks later on in the week.

"We'd like that," Rand declared as he helped Julie pick up their belongings. "See you later."

Julie waited until they were back on top of the cliff before she exploded. "How could you tell them we're married? How could you?"

"Because you couldn't seem to tell them that we're not," Rand countered, taking the keys out of her shaking hand to unlock the door.

Julie swept angrily inside, dropped her bundles on the floor, then turned around to face him. Rand stood calmly on the doorstep, making a slow job of dumping the sand out of his shoes. "Get in here!" she ordered cuttingly.

"Kind of bitchy for a new bride, aren't you?" Rand inquired as he stepped inside and closed the door behind him. "The last time we played house you never talked to me like that."

"The last time we played..." Julie screeched, temper soaring as she noted his smug grin, the one she'd always detested. "Five-year-old kids making believe they're married can't be compared with what you pulled today. I thought you'd changed but you haven't. You really enjoyed misleading those nice people."

His unrepentant smile never slipped an inch. "Nope. Playing house with you has always been one of my favorite games."

He dropped his sweatshirt and shoes beside Julie's beach bag, then went down on one knee. He rummaged around in the bag until he found his pipe and tobacco. Standing back up, he judged calmly, "I don't see what you're so upset about. My explanation will lead to the fewest questions."

Julie groaned and sank down on the couch. "This is awful, just awful. What if they saw us? Oh, Lord."

Rand sat down beside her, stretching his arm along the back of the couch. "What if they did? I'm sure they've seen people necking on the beach before."

"We were doing a lot more than necking and you know it," Julie snapped, crossing her arms and legs.

"Relax," Rand soothed. "You look as guilty as a kid caught with her hands in the cookie jar."

"That's apt, considering," Julie said in self-disgust.

Rand hooted with the humor he alone saw in the entendre.

"It is nothing to laugh about," she decreed, furious with herself for being unable to keep her eyes off the bare male chest heaving with mirth beside her. What was wrong with her, anyway? Even though he'd grown up into a sexy devil of a man, he was still Skeeter Maxwell—Skeeter the Cheater.

Unaware of her thoughts but responding to the naked desire he saw in her eyes, Rand slipped his arm around her and pulled her over to him. "Believe me, Julie—" he nibbled at her earlobe "—I wasn't laughing when we were down at the beach. I was too busy doing this."

His mouth was warm and moist and he caressed her with it, his breath soft along the column of her throat. He cradled her head in the crook of his arm and kissed her. As always her body yearned to respond, but this time she refused to give in to the feelings Rand aroused.

She broke away and stood up from the couch. "Don't. Don't start that again. I'm going back down there and right things with the Sellinghams." She started for the door.

Rand came after her. Catching her by the shoulders, he spun her around and enveloped her in his arms. "Trying to explain is what got us into this trouble."

He hauled her stiff body closer. "It doesn't really matter what they think, anyway. What matters is what we know about each other."

He ran his hands up and down her back, striving to relax her. He'd told himself on the beach to go slowly with her, but when she'd responded so quickly, he'd discovered he didn't possess that kind of control. As he saw it, the Sellinghams' arrival was merely an interruption. The fires had been hastily banked but could flame again with minimal stoking. With that end in mind, he kneaded and stroked, coaxing her body to yield.

She didn't relax and admitting temporary defeat, Rand reluctantly dropped his hands from her. "You think too much, Julie. You've got a big enough conscience for two people."

"It's a good thing I do because you don't have any," Julie vowed.

Putting greater space between them, making it easier to resist the temptation to step right back into his arms, she headed toward her bedroom. "As you told the Sellinghams, I do have work to do and I can't waste any more time today."

Rand's temper simmered just beneath the surface as he bit out, "Wasting time? What I want to do with you would never be a waste of time."

Without thinking, Julie retorted, "Well, that's a matter of opinion."

"What's wrong? Afraid I've finally become an expert at something you're not?"

"That remains to be seen," she hissed. "From what you've shown me so far, your technique could use some improvement. Now if you'll excuse me, I have work to do."

"Well, so do I," he growled and strode briskly past her. He paused at his bedroom door. "You can lie to yourself all you want but you certainly appeared to enjoy my technique. When you have a spare moment, maybe I can refresh your memory." With that, he entered his room and slammed the door behind him.

Slumping against the wall, Julie let out her pent-up breath. She'd never cared that her words might hurt him when they'd been children and argued over just about everything. But now she cared and wanted to follow him into his bedroom to apologize for wounding his ego. She'd been angry with herself so she'd lashed out at him.

She took one step in that direction, then pivoted and started toward her own bedroom. If she apologized she had no doubt just where they'd spend the next hour or so. He had been absolutely right about her enjoying his technique, but going to bed with Rand would be a mistake.

Rand was also right about their lovemaking not being a waste of time—she knew without a doubt it would be wonderful. However, they didn't know enough about each other as adults to leap into a physical relationship this fast. They might know all there was to know about the first thirteen years of their lives, but what about the fifteen after that?

The adult Rand Maxwell was almost a stranger to her, and Julie didn't fall into bed with strangers. She knew his age, his occupation and that he lived in New York. She knew he was single. But that information was as impersonal as a résumé and told her nothing about the inner man.

She peeled off her swimsuit, grabbed a robe and belted it snugly around her waist before heading toward the bathroom. Peeking out of her door, she listened. Hearing nothing, she assumed Rand was still sulking in his room.

After carefully locking the bathroom door behind her, Julie stepped into the shower stall and turned the tap on full blast. The water sluiced over her head, rinsing off the residue of salt from the ocean. She hoped it would also rinse off the memory of Rand's hands and mouth on her skin. But she discoverd it wasn't as easy to erase memories recorded by her senses as it was to wash the salt and sand from her skin.

As she dried off, she couldn't help looking in the mirror, half expecting to see signs on her body marking all the places he'd touched and kissed. Nothing was visible, of course, for his touch had been gentle, tender, loving. No, not loving. Loving encompassed far more than physical desire, and physical desire was all they felt for each other. Back in her room, she dressed quickly, then blow-dried her hair. Pushing all thought of the rapturous moments on the beach out of her mind, she went to work setting up her "office." Sweeping her cosmetics into a drawer, she determined that the top of the dressing table would serve nicely as a desk.

She was arranging the portable computer when she heard water running. Rand was taking a shower. Images of his naked body didn't help bolster her determination to spend the afternoon concentrating on her thesis. Volcanic activity suddenly seemed like very tame stuff compared to the fire ignited in her by one kiss from Rand.

She plopped down on a chair and inserted a master disk into the computer, then switched it on. After several seconds of quiet whirring, the computer was properly boosted and loaded with the word-processing program, and Julie inserted the second disk that contained her preliminary draft. She punched in a series of letters and waited for the information to appear on the screen. After several seconds a beep sounded and a message appeared on the monitor: "Syntax Error." *Not surprising*, Julie fumed. Her fingers were still trembling. She'd probably dropped a letter from the file name.

Clearing the screen, she tried again, only to be rewarded with another condemning beep and the "Syntax Error" message. It took three more attempts before the file loaded into the computer. By that time, Julie was so furious with herself she accidentally pushed a wrong button that cleared the screen and she had to start all over again.

She prayed frantically that she hadn't erased all the information on the disk. She'd made a copy as insurance against loss or damage, but that disk was safely stored in her apartment back in Los Angeles. It wouldn't be any good to her here in the middle of the Pacific Ocean.

The screen filled with words and Julie breathed a sigh of relief. It was all there. Turning to her printout, she started going through it, adding corrections and additions to the text in the computer. The first hour of work passed easily enough, for she didn't have to concentrate too hard. For the most part, she was editing what she'd already written. It was when she'd saved the text and loaded in a database program that she began to have trouble.

The telephone next to her bed was too far away from the dressing table to hook up the modem she needed to gain access to the data bank. She'd have to rearrange the furniture. It would have been easier to ask Rand for help in moving the heavy dresser, but she decided against it. She'd already had enough trouble blocking him from her mind.

After pushing and shoving and finally getting everything rearranged, Julie began to wonder how he could have ignored all the noise she'd made. "You'd think he'd be curious," she said aloud as she replaced her equipment on the makeshift desk.

Wiping away the sweat on her forehead, she grumbled, "With all those muscles, he could have picked up the darned thing and saved me a lot of trouble."

On the other hand, she was grateful he hadn't come to her aid. It was all those muscles that had scrambled her brains to begin with. The last thing she needed was another example of how weak she became when she was around him.

She was thirsty and hungry. A glance at her travel alarm told her it was long past lunchtime. She'd have to leave the safety of her room and possibly run into Rand in the kitchen. Maybe she'd just skip lunch. Her stomach growled and she realized she was acting like a child. She could certainly withstand seeing Rand again.

Remembering the vengeful streak in Rand when he'd been a youngster, yet unwilling to believe he would still resort to spite, she decided it was safe to emerge from her prison. Rand's door was still closed.

Unconsciously Julie tiptoed down the hallway and into the kitchen.

Cripes! She was doing it again. Sneaking around like a kid avoiding the school bully.

If Rand came out, he certainly wasn't going to pounce on her and prove what an expert lover he was. If he was anything like he'd been as a boy, he'd either gotten over his anger or devised some means of revenge that he'd spring on her when she was least expecting it. Whatever, at the moment she was probably safe. Not worrying about the noise she was making, she rummaged around in the refrigerator.

Rand still didn't appear and there was no sound from his room. Prepared for a confrontation, she was unreasonably disappointed by his continued self-imposed incarceration. She banged the cupboard doors rather loudly as she went about preparing her lunch.

Julie munched her sandwich in solitude, not tasting the mingled flavors of ham and cheese between slices of rye bread. Every few bites she leaned back in her chair and glanced down the hallway. Nothing. Nothing but silence. Maybe he'd fallen asleep. Possibly he was still suffering from jet lag. His night on the couch couldn't have been too restful.

She eyed the remnants of their breakfast that still cluttered the table. Legitimately it was her turn to clean up. He'd won their little race, even if he'd had to cheat to do it. Julie smiled to herself. She'd let him have his little triumph and maybe that would prove she'd changed. The young Julie would have rather died than admit defeat under questionable circumstances, but the adult Julie could give a little ground.

After loading the dishwasher and setting the kitchen to rights, Julie started back toward her own room. She was intent on spending the rest of the day working on her thesis. However, instead of turning right when she entered the short hallway, she turned left. She stood nervously before Rand's door, trying to decide if she should knock. She held her hand motionlessly in midair, cautiously weighing the advisability of her being the one to initiate a truce.

Rand couldn't possibly be asleep after all the racket she'd made in the kitchen, and the Rand she knew couldn't have become engrossed in anything for this length of time unless it was dangerous. Although it was reasonable to assume that as an adult his attention span had increased, she had serious doubts about that. There was far too much energy housed inside his big body for him to remain quietly and innocently in his room. She was almost positive he was plotting some sort of subtle and ingenious revenge for the way she'd talked to him.

She remembered a few of the more dastardly things he'd done to her in the past. She'd beat him at a game of one on one; he'd let the air out of every inflatable she owned. She'd taken first place in track on field day; he'd filled her running shoes with Jell-O.

She decided to confront him now and get it over with. Heaven only knew what he might devise for her if she left him alone too long. She rapped on the door then took a step backward, bracing herself for whatever mood he might be in. She even rehearsed a few opening comments as she waited.

Hi there. Thought you might like some lunch. Maybe the truth would be better. *Rand. I can't stand*

it any longer. Are you still mad at me? No good. If
he answered yes, she'd be on the defensive. Better to
take the initiative. *Listen here. Let's talk this out like
adults and quit skulking around like kids.*

There was still no evidence of life coming from the
other side of the slab of wood. Hesitantly she
reached for the knob and slowly turned it. Opening
the door just a crack, she peered in. All she could see
was the bed and it was empty though the spread was
slightly rumpled.

Stealthily Julie pushed the door wider, sure that
at any moment, Rand would come into view. The
room was empty! A towel lay crumpled in the middle of the floor. Several items of clothing were
draped across one of the chairs. An empty suitcase
lay open on the luggage rack in one corner, evidence that Rand had unpacked, but the man was
nowhere in sight.

Unable to help herself, she picked up the towel and
immediately wished she hadn't. It was damp and
smelled like Rand. She breathed deeply. It seemed
as if the whole room smelled of him. The rich blend
of men's cologne, soap and pipe tobacco sent her
senses spinning. She dropped the towel.

Turning on her heel, Julie retraced her steps. A
quick look out one of the windows confirmed that
his rental car was gone. She must have been in the
midst of dragging furniture around when he'd driv-
en away.

"Could've had the decency to let me know he was
going out," she muttered as she headed toward her
room. "I've been driving myself crazy over nothing. If we're going to be stuck sharing this place,
we're going to have to set up some rules."

Back in her own room, she plopped down in front of the computer. She punched in the necessary codes and waited for the information to come through from the computer bank at the research center in California. For a while she was able to focus her attention on compiling the information, but eventually the figures began to run together.

"I should put on my glasses," she mumbled to herself, but instead, propped her elbows on the table and her chin on the heels of her hands.

Rand's scent floated into her nostrils. His face replaced the images on the monitor. Unconsciously she ran her palms down her arms, wishing it was Rand's hands on her. The ache she'd felt on the beach returned.

"Snap out of it, Julie!" she sternly reprimanded, forcing herself to pay attention to the sentences slowly scrolling up the screen.

Everything was fine until she began delving into submarine eruptions in the Pacific and came across a reference to "pillow lavas." She couldn't conjure up any images of the rounded lava forms. Instead, she saw Rand's head on a soft, down-filled pillow. Her head pillowed on his broad chest, his head pillowed on her breasts. His body pillowed over hers and vice versa.

"Go to bed with the man and relieve this frustration," Julie advised aloud, her fingers nimbly moving over the keyboard, unwittingly typing the order onto the screen.

"Face it lady. You're never going to get any work done unless you do something about this situation. Once you get all this pent-up sexual energy out of your system, maybe you can get your dissertation finished."

Realizing it was useless to work any longer, she punched the Save button on the keyboard, and once the process was completed, turned off the machine.

5

"IF I WERE THE TYPE TO SAY I told you so," Will Stites remarked as he left the kitchen. "I'd repeat it twice so both of you would think before doing anything so thoughtless again."

"Is he always right?" Sylvia Maxwell made a face at her co-author, then stared morosely into her coffee cup. "I feel terrible about this, just terrible. When I talked to Rand, he said he and Julie weren't even speaking."

"I can't understand it," Angela lowered her chin into her hands and emitted an unhappy sigh. "Real people are so unreliable. Everytime we set up an arranged marriage in our books, it turns out so well. All the handsome hero has to do is set eyes on the beautiful maiden and he's a goner. What's wrong with those two? Can't they see that they're meant for each other?"

The question went unanswered for so long that Angela was sure her partner felt too despondent to respond. Therefore, she jumped almost an inch off her chair when Sylvia let out a loud, joyous yelp. "Not to worry, my dear," she advised breezily. "The course of true love never runs smooth. We've forgotten the scenario and we're the ones who wrote it."

At Angela's perplexed look, she went on, "Don't you see? This was inevitable. Do our heroes ever admit straight off that they've fallen head over heels in love with our lovely heroine? Of course, they don't. The hero makes life miserable for the heroine until he's reached the point of desperation, then he swallows his male pride and admits he can't go on without her. Patience old friend. There's still plenty of time for that to happen. I know Rand. He can only go so long before he takes action."

Angela was still not convinced. "I don't know, Syl. You're forgetting what Julie's like. Beneath that Gainsborough face is the most stubborn wench ever born. I think Will might be right. We may have set up something that will backfire on us all. You and I might think Rand and Julie were destined from the cradle to be together but we may very well be wrong. If we are, we've managed to give our children the worst two weeks of their lives. I doubt they'll be too grateful."

"Rand didn't sound very grateful," Sylvia admitted, her beatific expression replaced with an anxious frown. "He swore at me. My mouth almost dropped through the floor. Not once, when he was growing up did he ever speak to me like that."

"What did he say?" Angela asked, though she was quite sure she didn't want to hear it.

"He said, 'My God, mother, you've really done it this time.'"

"I don't know about you, Syl, but when Julie comes home for a visit, if she ever does again, I'm pleading temporary insanity."

Grimly, Sylvia concurred, "Maybe we can get adjoining cells in the booby hatch."

"I'm sure Will would be quite happy to make the arrangements," Angela concluded miserably.

RAND RESTED HIS ARMS along the back of the bench, his fingertips brushing the worn wood. The monkeypod tree above him spread its wide branches like an umbrella against the sun. Nearby, two older men shared a bench, talking quietly. Beyond them, upon a blanket laid out across the grass, a baby laughed and cooed as a young girl watched over him. Few of the benches scattered beneath the protection of the ancient tree were empty, yet it was quiet. Hushed and musical voices buffered the sounds of traffic along Kahului's main avenue.

The spot was said to be a favorite gathering place for locals and Rand hoped to absorb some of their easygoingness by sitting among them. He'd driven across the isthmus of the island, hoping the rough and jagged terrain, the different scenery of the windward side, would help him divert his thoughts. It hadn't helped much.

The deep-blue water in Kahului Harbor reminded him too much of Julie's eyes. Wandering around the three shopping centers along Kaahumanu Avenue was too reminiscent of their meeting in Honolulu. Stupidly, he'd gone into a bookstore on the pretext of buying a newspaper and found himself standing in front of a rack of romance novels. He'd remembered all too vividly how he'd swept Julie into his arms and the passionate way she'd responded. In his haste to get out of the store, he'd nearly forgotten to make his purchase.

He should go back he thought. The way he and Julie had been avoiding each other for the past three days hadn't done either of them any good. Rand felt as taut as a bow string and from the way Julie jumped whenever he entered a room, the excrutiat-

ingly polite way she spoke to him, he could tell that
she felt the same way.

The urge to toss her down on the nearest bed and
make love to her had become the overriding moti-
vation of his life, but he'd be damned if he'd admit
that to her. Instead, he'd chosen to stay away from
the villa for long hours, eliminating the possibility
that he'd be the one to breach the ever-widening gap
that had developed between them. Nevertheless,
she'd have to come to her senses soon; this waiting
was killing him and he wasn't going out alone.

Rand could have driven back across the narrow
neck of the island but he decided to drive around the
western tip. The longer drive would give him more
time to think, more time to devise some way to get
beyond the impasse, which, he had to admit, was not
all Julie's doing.

However, once he was a mile or so down the road,
he had something much more pressing to think
about: survival. The steep, unpaved, winding road
between Kahului Bay and Honolua was an axle
breaker. Controlling his vehicle took all of his skill
and concentration. If he wasn't careful, he'd wind up
in the Pacific Ocean or wrapped around a palm tree.
His teeth were already rattling so violently he feared
that years of orthodontia were in jeopardy.

At Nakalele Point, he stopped to recover from the
rough ten miles he'd traveled. Off the road and out
from behind the wheel, he let the beauty of weathered sandstone bluffs and the picturesque light-
house at the island's north point calm his jangled
nerves. Leaning against the front fender of his car,
he began to think more clearly than he had since that
day on the beach.

After their stupid argument, he'd needed to put some space between himself and Julie. A shower hadn't helped cool him down—her scent had filled the bathroom. Trying to bury himself in his study of Euro-Asian politics had been equally useless. He'd found himself attempting to apply the negotiation concepts he'd studied to his relationship with Julie, rather than sketching an outline for his new course. After half an hour, he'd given up and left the condominium. Three days later, he still hadn't done any worthwhile work.

Caution, compromise and patience. Weren't they the keys to any successful negotiations? Perhaps he could apply those concepts to Julie after all, if he kept a level head. He'd wasted a lot of time and they only had two weeks. Back in his car, he continued on to Lahaina, his strategy for winning Julie over forming rapidly in his mind.

Phase one was put into motion when he stopped at the Oceanhouse on Lahaina's historic Front Street and made reservations in the upstairs dining room. Assured of a table next to the windows, Rand returned to his car and headed toward Maalaea, impatient to get back to the villa.

Phase two involved convincing her to go to dinner with him. That might not be as easy but they both had to eat. Julie had certainly made it clear that she didn't intend to provide his meals. For the past few days, he'd subsisted on pineapples and peanut butter sandwiches.

He didn't know what Julie had been eating. The kitchen was always scrupulously clean whenever he entered it. She hadn't even provided him with any leftovers. Maybe she was no more skilled in the kitchen than he was. If so, it shouldn't take much to persuade her that going out to dinner was preferable to their eating anything either one of them could prepare.

Phase three should fall easily into place during the meal. He would be charming, a fascinating conversationalist and a wonderful listener. By the time coffee was served, she'd know all there was to know about his present life and he hers.

Phase four. Now here was where caution and patience came in. Just because they were sharing a hide-a-way in the midst of Paradise, that was no reason to get carried away. That their being together was set up by their parents was even more reason not to indulge in a casual affair. Their romantic-minded mothers believed strongly in the one man, one woman, happily-ever-after theory and if he was going to come across as the perfect hero, he'd have to think with his brain rather than the other more selfish parts of his anatomy.

After all, his feelings toward Julie were far from casual and she deserved more than a fling that lasted no longer than the length of their stay. She was beautiful, stunning, but his attraction to her was prompted by more than the obvious surface dressing. He couldn't find words to describe his feelings toward her, what exactly drew him so strongly but, whatever they were, they were basic.

Maybe it came down to a primal recognition of one's mate. That idea should have been frightening to a man who had thought he was thoroughly enjoying being single, but it wasn't. Julie had awakened something deep within him and he wasn't about to let it die or kill it with his own blundering.

For a while, at least, their physical attraction for each other needed to be kept at bay. He smacked the steering wheel with the palm of his hand. "Right again Stilts!" he pronounced. "This time ol' Skeeter the Cheater will play fair."

He and Julie did need to spend some time getting reaquainted before they became lovers. Friendship first. He'd go by her rules but for once he knew the object of the game and she didn't. If he played his cards right, he couldn't lose.

By the time Rand turned into the drive leading to their condominium complex, he was convinced his strategy was sound. He'd gone over every detail, leaving nothing to chance. "Find out what she's been doing with her life and tell her about yours," he reminded himself under his breath as he parked his car alongside Julie's

"Your first objective is to find out what makes the adult Julie tick." He tossed his keys into the air and caught them with one hand. With a victorious whoop, he bounded up the steps.

Julie was gone. Rand sensed it the moment he entered the villa. Her bedroom door was open but the room empty. After a brief moment of panic, he consoled himself that she hadn't gone far since her car was parked outside. However, the thought that she might have gone down to the bay for a swim was no consolation.

"You little idiot!" he grumbled as he tore off his clothes and pulled on his swim trunks. Where was her infamous caution when she most needed it? He didn't know what kind of undertow was out there, but he was certain even a strong swimmer like Julie shouldn't be swimming by herself.

She'd taken the same swimming lessons that he had. Didn't she remember the buddy system? There were rules for this sort of thing and she of all people should be following them! If anything happened to her he'd...

Rand tore down the winding path to the beach in record time. Running at top speed, his body's momentum carried him forward but his feet were slowed by the sifting sand of the beach. Stumbling, he tried frantically to keep his balance.

He fell hard. Stunned, gasping for breath, sputtering sand from his mouth, Rand scanned the beach and the water for signs of Julie. Nothing. Feeling more foolish than relieved, Rand rolled to his back, pulling the fresh ocean air into his lungs.

"Should've known," he muttered. "Stilts always plays by the rules."

Being prepared was another one of her favorite philosophies. And retired Girl Scout that she was, she would never have come to the beach without a bag full of gear. The beach was empty except for the palm trees mocking him with their long, waving fronds.

The climb back up to the top of the cliff was slower and more painful. He hadn't worn shoes. He'd been too panicked on his way down to notice that the crushed shells and gravel were wreaking havoc with the soles of his feet. On the return trip, however, every step reminded him of his earlier folly. Limping, he cursed himself, the path and Julie every inch of the way.

His humor didn't improve when he finally reached the clearing and was immediately hailed from the concealing shadows of one of the front lanais.

"Rand. Your wife's over here. Come join us for the drink we promised you," Gene Sellingham invited.

"Julie's with you?"

"We've been showing her our half of the villa. Glad we came out when we did and spotted you," Gene relayed. "Been for a swim?"

"Not exactly," Rand responded. He gritted his teeth but managed to walk without revealing his suffering. Knowing it would be boorish to turn down an invitation he'd already accepted, he mounted the steps. Moving slowly but maintaining his poise, he hoped he wasn't leaving behind a telltale trail of bloodied footprints.

Rand held out his hand to Gene Sellingham, nodded and smiled at the man's wife. *Candace, wasn't that her name?* He'd been so preoccupied for the past few days, he was surprised he remembered their existence, let alone their names. Gamely, he lowered himself to one end of the settee, glowering at Julie who occupied the other.

A gold storm of fury lit up his eyes. He'd practically killed himself and all the while, she'd been safely next door with the Sellinghams. He gave her the barest semblance of a smile, supposedly in greeting but it was no greeting at all. It was a threat. *Just wait till I get you home.*

Julie arched one brow at the unmistakable irritation in Rand's eyes. She couldn't help but notice that his bare chest was coated with a powder of white sand and the skin was red and blotchy, but she couldn't imagine what that had to do with her. His trunks were dry and the only moisture she saw was the sweat beading his forehead and clinging to the damp strands of his brown hair. Evidently, he'd just gone a few rounds with the sandy beach—and lost.

Unable to resist, she observed, "Most people prefer to body surf in the water."

Rand didn't dignify that comment with an answer. Turning to Gene, he inquired, "You folks been enjoying yourselves?"

He kept his feet planted firmly on the floor, ignoring Julie. He'd be damned if he was going to admit the wretched condition of his feet to anyone—especially her. She'd never let him hear the end of it. It was enough that she'd surmised he'd taken a header in the sand.

"Here, young fella," Gene said jovially as he thrust a tall, frosted glass in Rand's gritty hand. "You look like you could use one of these."

"Thanks." Rand grasped the glass like a lifeline and consumed half its contents in one smooth swallow. Too late, he realized his mistake. The rum-dominated mixture hit his stomach like an out-of-control locomotive.

Rand's mind formed an instant picture of a cartoon character. He felt like Wiley Coyote consuming something so potent that his stomach bounced to the floor then ricocheted to his chin and knocked him out. It was all he could do to keep from choking.

Julie had to push the tip of her tongue against the inside of her cheek to keep from laughing. Rand's eyes were watering and his reddened face was paralyzed with the shock. "Gene mixes a mean Zombie, don't you think Rand?"

In a preadolescent voice, Rand agreed. "He certainly does." He was forced to stop and clear his throat before he could utter another word. "Best I've ever had."

Right then, he considered the strong drink better suited to pouring over his feet than to drink. He was sure there was enough alcohol in the concoction to cleanse his wounds more thoroughly than the strongest antiseptic known to medical science. It was already eating holes in his empty stomach and he had the awful feeling the alcohol would soon move on up to his empty head.

"Too bad you were gone all afternoon, Rand," Julie said solicitously but her sincerity was ruined by the amusement in her eyes. "My mother called a little while ago. I told her to convey to your mother just what we thought about the accommodations."

Exactly what Julie had had her mother convey was not lost on Rand. He'd done the same with his mother the day before. At least, there was one subject on which they could both agree. Being the only children of Angel Silver was sometimes a real trial. For the first time in three days they exchanged real smiles.

It's a start, Rand thought, as he warmed himself in the sparkle of her eyes. Now if he could just get past her anger over the lies he'd told the Sellinghams, maybe things could get rolling again. In the next second, he learned that she'd not only forgiven him but had decided to get in the spirit of the game.

"I don't know if we've told you that this trip was a gift from our parents," she explained. "As I said earlier, Rand's mother is the Sylver half of Angel Sylver and my mom's the Angel half. They're born romantics so you can imagine how concerned they were that we'd like this place."

"I doubt there's a more romantic spot on the face of the earth." Candace glanced at her husband, her tone growing dreamy as her gaze returned to Julie.

"I know of one," Julie supplied, an impish glint sparking in her eyes. Candace had just provided her with a wonderful opening. She'd spent the past hour juggling the Sellinghams's questions concerning her mythical marriage to Rand. Now he could see what it felt like to squirm over a lie. "Nothing could be more romantic than that cruise we took to Acapulco. Could it, darling?"

"Come again?" Rand asked, his eyes flickering like newly lit candles.

"He doesn't like admitting what a hopeless romantic he is," Julie said conspiratorially. "You'll never believe how we got married, Candace."

Savoring Rand's incredulous expression, she continued, "The story could have come right off the pages of one of our mother's books. Don't you think so, Rand?"

"Er, something like that," Rand mumbled to Julie's delight.

"It was purely coincidence that we were on the cruise." Julie warmed to the fictional tale. "But then, like two lonely ships passing in the night, we found each other. It was fate. Beneath a tropical moon, we were rewarded by destiny's promise."

While Rand choked on his drink, Julie expounded, "I'll never forget the night he proposed to me. He sang beautiful love songs beneath my stateroom window. He sounded so lonely, so desperate, almost begging me to marry him. No woman on earth could have refused."

"That is romantic," Candace enthused. "You must have a remarkable voice, Rand."

"It's truly unforgettable," Julie agreed, slanting Rand an exaggeratedly adoring gaze.

"You'll have to sing for us sometime," Candace urged.

It was all Rand could do to keep his laughter inside. It would serve Julie right if he burst into song. His voice was certainly unforgettable; he sounded like a bull frog croaking underwater. However, what he lacked in talent, he'd always made up for in enthusiasm. When he could finally look at Julie without breaking up, he sensed she was remembering the same childhood incident that had come into his mind at the mention of his singing.

The Maxwells and the Stites had attended a church service together and after the first line of "Amazing Grace" his mother had told him to have the grace to keep quiet. He could still see Julie, looking like an angel in a pale pink dress, hiding her giggles behind the lacey white gloves on her small hands. For the rest of the service, he'd doodled ugly pictures of her on the back of his bulletin and taken great joy in showing them to her on the car ride home.

"I'm afraid my singing is a pleasure reserved for my wife," Rand apologized, giving Julie a look that would have melted metal. "I know I sound good to her, but that's only because she loves me so much."

"How sweet." Candace sighed and this time Julie was the one who choked on her drink.

"Julie thinks so." Rand grinned.

Julie swallowed the gigantic lump in her throat. She had hoped to treat Rand to a little of his own medicine but he was not only swallowing it, but enjoying it immensely. She gave up trying to beat him at his own game and diverted the conversation to safer topics. "Have you been to Lahaina yet, Candace?"

Rand hid a grin, not daring to let Julie see the satisfaction he felt. Though in the end she'd retreated, he was relieved that they were finally back on speaking terms. He took her teasing as a good omen for the future. All of his previous ill temper was forgotten. As soon as he'd removed himself from the list of walking wounded, he was going to put phase two of his campaign into action and be the well deserving recipient of some very positive results.

A blissful smile turned up the corners of his mouth and he leaned back on the wicker settee. He began to brush the dried sand off his body, feeling much more like his usual laid-back self. He grinned at Gene as he took a second, much more cautious, sip of his drink.

He closed his eyes and took a deep breath of flower-scented air. A cool breeze wafted through the palms and soothed the irritating scrapes on his elbows and knees. Off in the distance he could hear the sound of the waves slapping like foamy fans upon the beach. The sound was beautiful. This whole place was beautiful. Life was beautiful.

Having been listening with only half an ear to the conversation between Julie and the Sellinghams, Rand's inner radar suddenly started bleeping warning signals.

"We'd love to have you and Rand join us, Julie," Candace was inviting.

"Nothing like a good steak, eh Rand?" Gene commented, filling Rand's glass again. "The Steak House in Wailea ought to be just the ticket, don't you think? I'd bet a big strapping boy like you would prefer something he could sink his teeth into."

Gene started to pour more of the potent drink into Julie's glass but she smoothly demurred. Undaunted by her refusal, he confided, "I for one have had enough seafood, rice and tropical fruit dishes. What do ya say? Meet back here in about an hour?"

"That sounds—"

"Lovely," Rand finished for Julie. "Unfortunately, we already have reservations in Lahaina for this evening."

Rising from the settee, he reached for Julie and pulled her along with him. "I'm sure you'll understand if we make dinner together another time. And thanks again for the drink. You'll have to give us the recipe. That is unless it's a secret."

Unceremoniously, Rand hustled Julie across the lanai and down the steps. "Sorry we have to run but we'll have to get a move on or we'll lose our table."

"Did you have to be so rude?" Julie demanded as soon as they were safely beyond earshot of the Sellinghams.

Rand didn't slow his limping stride or loosen his hold on her elbow. They rounded the corner of the villa and were mounting the short flight of steps to their door before he answered. "Rude? Me? I wasn't rude, only truthful."

He opened the door and pushed Julie inside. "We do have reservations and we'll lose our table if we don't hurry. You want the bathroom first?"

"Halt!" Julie wrenched her arm from Rand's grasp and firmly planted her feet. "I don't recall being asked to go out anywhere."

"Will you please do me the honor of having dinner with me at the Carthaginian Bar at the Oceanhouse?" Rand politely invited, hoping to erase the stubborn expression on her face. Rand knew that look all too well. He'd made a tactical error and he knew better. He'd made plans that included Julie without consulting her first.

"Are you giving me any choice?" she asked, blue eyes like gleaming bayonets pointed at his face.

"I'm sorry, Julie," he apologized in his most humble and sincere manner. He was rewarded for his effort by a visible softening of her attitude. Apologies had always gone a long way with Julie. She preferred thinking she was in charge but was willing to accept mistakes if they were freely admitted by the transgressor.

This idea about getting to know each other better was beginning to seem pretty ridiculous. Hadn't he read somewhere that a child's personality was set by age three? He knew Julie almost as well as he knew himself.

What he had to do was use that knowledge to serve his own ends. Whatever he didn't know about her was probably superficial and unimportant anyway. Still, he was determined to play this game by her rules if only to say that he could. It was the only way to win with her and win he would.

Julie's birthday was in August. That made her a Leo. Remembering what little he knew about the astrological signs, Rand threw himself on the mercy of the noble monarch, adding his dimpled charm for good measure.

"I thought you'd rather go out than chance partaking of my culinary skills. You fixed my breakfast that first day and it seemed only fair that I return the favor. I'll provide dinner tonight."

Craning his head around the corner, he spied the clock in the kitchen. Actually they had more than enough time to meet their reservations but when the Sellinghams had started including them in their evening plans, Rand had seen phase two of his campaign going right out to sea. Phases two and three centered on an intimate *tête-à-tête*, not a foursome.

"Actually, I've heard of the Oceanhouse and I've wanted to see Lahaina," Julie admitted slowly, her calm tone in direct conflict with her thoughts.

An evening spent alone with Rand would be far more likely to end the way she wanted it to than if they'd gone out with the Sellinghams. These past three days had been the longest ones in her life. Sharing the villa with him, yet sticking with the hands-off policy she had insisted upon, had become sheer torture. Enough was enough.

Her pulse rate had taken a dramatic leap the moment she'd seen Rand emerge from the path. Now, faced with all that naked, muscled flesh of his, it was almost more than she could do to keep herself from dragging him off to the nearest bedroom and having her way with him. He'd developed so nicely, aged so beautifully, matured so wonderfully well.

He was looking at her with that crooked grin of his, boyish yet appraising, and Julie felt all the bones in her body begin to dissolve. He turned up the gold voltage in his eyes and all of her muscles began to melt as well. As her mother would have put it, she was a goner.

Lord, if Rand had any idea what the sight of him in nothing but a brief swimsuit did to her, she'd never hear the last of it. She was either a prude, by Rand's definition, or had suddenly developed an obsession for the male body. No, not every male body —just Rand's.

"Then you'll go?" Rand asked, boyish hope tinging both the smile and his voice.

"I'll go," Julie verified, a mischievous glint in her eyes as she breezed past Rand on the way to her bedroom. "I'll even let you have the bathroom first."

Before Rand could respond to her magnanimous gesture, she teased, "All that sand must be uncomfortable, to say nothing of the state of your poor feet. You really should tend to them."

"Aren't you even curious to know how I got in this condition?" Rand inquired casually.

"After all these years, I've learned its better not to ask when you show up looking like a wounded knight returning from battle."

Rand rather liked that analogy. He had been wounded trying to rescue his lady love from the jaws of death. The fact that she hadn't been there to benefit from his heroic efforts was purely incidental.

Mellowed by rum, Julie's acceptance of his invitation and her romantic description of him, Rand's mouth curved into a silly grin. The grin was still there when Julie ducked behind her bedroom door then chided, "Try to remember to wear shoes the next time you joust with that path. Otherwise you may not rise to joust another day."

"Fear not, fair lady," Rand misquoted back, "I'm a little wounded but am not slain. I will lay me down to bleed a short while but soon will rise to meet you yet again."

6

THE CARTHAGINIAN BAR was ideal, Julie thought as she finished a cup of Hawaii's famous Kona coffee. The entire meal had been delicious and beautifully served. The atmosphere was quiet, romantic. On the second floor, their secluded corner table looked out across the floodlit breakers below. Music played by a group on the first floor filtered softly up the stairs.

Relics from old ships adorned the walls, reminders of the colorful past when Lahaina had been a whaling port. Imagining that time had been easy as she and Rand had driven through the town. Weathered frame buildings had been restored to give the flavor of nineteenth-century Nantucket rather than twentieth-century Hawaii.

No less a part of the atmosphere was the man seated across from Julie. Wearing an open-collared white shirt, navy pants that emphasized his lean hips and strong thighs, Rand was the romaticized image of a whaling captain. His dark hair fell in waves across his forehead. Occasional streaks of copper in the chestnut depths proved he'd spent a lot of time outdoors. She could picture his white teeth flashing in his bronzed face as he braved the elements, laughing as the sea spray hit his face.

Unfortunately sharing a meal with the most striking-looking man in the restaurant didn't nec-

essarily add up to a romantic interlude—far from it.
To Julie's dismay, though their relationship wasn't
as strained as it had been for the past three days,
there was no apparent sparkle of awareness on
Rand's part. He was behaving as if they were just two
old friends discussing their activities since they'd last
seen each other.

His attitude toward her was light-years away from
what it had been the morning he had proclaimed
them newlyweds to the Sellinghams. Julie supposed
she had no one to blame but herself for that. She'd
made it perfectly clear what she thought about his
fictitious honeymoon idea and insisted that their relationship be platonic. After these past few days of
mounting frustration she had hoped this dinner date
would bring about a change in their relationship.
Unfortunately, as the evening progressed, nothing
had happened to indicate that would be the case.

She'd thought the strapless sheath she'd chosen to
wear would have warranted some comment, but
Rand seemed not to notice how the silky peacock-
blue fabric matched her eyes and complemented her
skin. She'd taken such pains with her preparations
and makeup. Her lips glistened with a dewy gloss,
her eyes were enhanced with a smoky-blue shadow
and mascara. She'd brushed her hair into a shim-
mering golden fall that swung freely below her
shoulders. A liberal amount of *Magie Noire* had
been applied to most of her body, but the man was
totally oblivious to all the feminine lures she'd
employed.

He looked the same, but he definitely wasn't the
same man who'd confessed just three days ago that
her body drove him wild. Tonight when he'd

stopped at a street-side vendor and purchased a lei for her, she'd expected him to accompany the presentation with at least the traditional light kiss. Instead, he'd unceremoniously dropped the necklace of vanda orchids over her head and then promptly steered her into the restaurant.

All through dinner he had behaved like a sterotyped college professor—dignified and circumspect. Through her mother and his, she'd known he was on the staff at Columbia University but would never have believed he could carry off the role of the intellectual so well. From what she remembered of his childhood character, she would have thought he'd be a rebel who took pleasure in undermining the foundations of the ivory towers.

Instead, his demeanor this evening and his discussion of his work indicated he was very conservative in his viewpoints. He even served on a presidential advisory council on Eurasian politics. Only in his teaching methods might he be considered at all liberal.

From his description, Julie gained the distinct impression that he conducted his classes in an extremely informal manner. More times than not, it seemed he shunned the lecture hall assigned to him, preferring to meet with his students outside when the weather permitted. Or he'd hold class in student hangouts where he encouraged debate and welcomed student suggestions for course material.

"I want them to experience democracy, not just listen to me tell them all I know," Rand revealed, growing more animated as he described his classes. "My theory is that they should be their own teachers with me functioning primarily as a guide. It's exciting to see them really sink their teeth into an issue and run with it."

Shaking her head, Julie reflected on his obvious enjoyment of the education process. "When we were kids, you seemed to hate school and spent as little time attending as you could get away with. I just can't imagine you surrounded by books and doing something so staid as teaching political science—Dr. Maxwell."

"Political science is far from staid, my dear soon-to-be Dr. Stites," Rand responded with mock affrontery.

Calling upon every ounce of control he'd accumulated over the years, he adopted his best lecture-hall tone and demeanor. It wasn't easy. Her perfume, the scent of her shampoo and the way her thick hair swung against her shoulders with every movement of her head were steadily eroding all his good intentions. And those eyes...A man could lose himself in their mysterious depths.

The orchid lei he'd given her draped across her bare shoulders and caressed her smooth skin. The string of delicate blossoms lay across her breasts, rising and falling with each breath she took, calling his attention continually to the curved fullness above the edge of her dress. The knowledge that only one narrow length of elastic held up that dress had been driving him slowly insane since the minute she'd emerged from her bedroom at the start of the evening. He'd just have to curl one fingertip under the shirred edge and push down to free those soft, lush...

Rand cleared his throat and shifted in his chair. "If I may quote Aristotle a little loosely, politics is the most important of human activities. It's one of the means by which people seek to understand the human condition and man's fate."

Political science had nothing to do with understanding his condition, Rand thought dismally. Human physiology would be a more appropriate field of study to explain it. He could only hope that his chosen field might help him determine his future. It had already shown him a way to be the master of his own fate—or so he hoped.

"What do you do in your spare time?" Julie asked, again forcing Rand to dominate their conversation. She reached for the small glass of Kahlua that had accompanied her coffee, hoping the liqueur would numb her senses, calm her nerves.

Rand grabbed at her question, gazing beyond her to keep from falling into a trance at the sight of her soft, kissable lips lightly touching the delicate crystal glass. Active conversation. That was the best way to keep his mind off Julie and what her presence across the table was doing to him. Besides, the sooner all this information was imparted, the sooner they'd get to Phase Four. Arriving there very soon was becoming of primary importance.

"I spend most of my spare time at a recreation center for children with learning disabilities," he divulged. "I coach a basketball team of twelve- and thirteen-year-olds."

Julie choked on her drink. "You're a coach?"

"I'll have you know that since we last met on a basketball court, I've mastered a few good moves. One of these days we'll have to get together again and see who nets what," he replied enigmatically.

"I can't picture you dealing with a bunch of kids."

"Takes a hyper kid to understand one," Rand confessed with a wry grin. "Most of them have way above-average intelligence but can't learn in traditional ways. They're often frustrated because of it. Once their problems are recognized and an educational program tailored for them, they do well. However, they usually carry some emotional scars and need to be around someone who understands, someone who's been there.

"You see, my problems didn't start when my dad died." Tamping tobacco into his pipe's bowl, he relaxed back into his chair. "I never was able to really control myself."

"That's an understatement," Julie inserted, but there was no condemnation in her tone. "You haven't changed much," she teased, hoping to arouse the exciting man who'd held her, kissed her and caressed her.

Rand raised one brow then cleared his throat. "Dad understood and knew how to handle me because he'd been the same way when he was a kid," he stated, safely avoiding her entendre. "Mom did her best by me but she just couldn't do it all by herself. Besides, I was so damned angry that my father died, I went a little berserk for a while."

"That must have been a difficult time for you." She leaned forward, reached across the table and covered his hand with hers. The memory of a thirteen-year-old Rand, uncharacteristically subdued and dressed in a suit, came to mind. They had all been stunned by his father's sudden death. A massive heart attack with no warning and no chance of survival had struck him down in the very prime of life.

"I liked your dad. We all shared your loss," Julie said sincerely, realizing so clearly now, years later, how very desolate Rand had been. "I wish you could have talked about it back then, maybe I could've understood some of what you were feeling."

Rand swallowed and blinked, surprised to be reacting so emotionally after all these years. He'd dealt with his loss and thought it no longer affected him. "Thanks Julie, but I had to work it out myself. As I recall, you tried."

He turned his palm up and laced his fingers through hers. Studying their interwoven hands, he said, "I remember the day of his funeral, you came up and stood beside me and started to say something nice."

Looking straight into her eyes, his own soft and warm, he asked softly, "Do you remember?"

"Yes, I wanted to tell you how unfair I thought it was," Julie answered just as softly, drawn by the tenderness and vulnerability in his gaze. "But you ran away before I could say how sorry I was you couldn't have had him longer."

"Do you know why I ran away?"

"No."

"I didn't want to cry in front of you and I was jealous," he stated, never breaking his gaze.

"Jealous?" Julie asked, comprehending that he might not have wanted to shed his tears in front of her. But jealous? Of what?

"You still had a father, and it seemed like the final straw." His fingers tightened slightly around hers. "You had everything I wanted: height, athletic ability, good grades. And most of all, a dad. At that moment, I think I hated you."

Embarrassed at how intense he'd become, he relaxed his grip and gave her a lopsided smile of apology. "My feelings didn't last long and it wasn't your fault." He let go of her hand, pushed away from the table and rose.

"Let's go for a walk," he invited as he pulled out her chair. "I'll explain what or rather who pulled me out of my self-pity and set me straight."

As they walked along Front Street, Rand caught Julie's hand. He held her slender palm and fingers lightly but firmly. It felt possessive but comfortable, and Julie enjoyed the feeling.

At first, each evidently lost in private thoughts, they walked along the street making only occasional desultory remarks. His reasons for working with children revealed so much about him. Rand was a far more sensitive and caring person than she would ever have given him credit for. She condemned herself for being so shallow; she hadn't recognized those traits in him when they'd been youngsters.

Rand resembled his late father in many ways. His height, hair color, even the way he smiled. Randall Maxwell had been graced with those same deep, slashing dimples in his cheeks and the tiny laugh lines bracketing his eyes.

Julie began to remember many things about the man, especially that she'd always felt comfortable around him. He'd been so energetic, fun to be around, had even teased her, but there had always been an underlying gentleness and warmth about him. Perhaps that was why Sylvia had never remarried. Maybe no other man could measure up, and after having been Randall Maxwell II's wife for fiteen years, she wouldn't settle for second best.

Suddenly Julie knew why she thought Rand was so much more attractive than the bronzed beachboys who populated Waikiki Beach. The inner man dominated the outer shell. It was that inner man who held far more potent appeal for her than all the muscle and handsome features that formed the shell.

How could she have missed Rand's inner worth? Weren't the eyes supposed to be mirrors of the soul? Rand's eyes had always fascinated her, but she'd ignored their message until now. The glittering amber star against the field of deep brown seemed so symbolic of his character. Sparkling life mixed with rich depth. The blend attracted her and frightened her at the same time.

A vacation fling with Rand wouldn't be wise. Intimacy with a man like him would not be something to take lightly nor to forget easily. She'd never had a casual affair before, why on earth she had thought it advisable now, Julie couldn't fathom.

Yet when he dropped her hand and moved his own to the small of her back to guide her down Papelekane Street and toward the harbor, her doubts gave way to the fantasy. If she had an affair with Rand, she'd have some wonderful memories. She might not have him longer than their stay on Maui, but wouldn't those few days of ecstasy be worth the pain of losing him?

Oh, you're a masochist, Julie Stites, she condemned, but wondered fleetingly if she was falling victim to the islands' atmosphere and philosophies. *Hoomanawanui.* This night was beautiful. This man was beautiful. Why even consider tomorrow? But, caution again waved its flag through her conscience, causing her to examine her motives and the greater implications of such a step.

"Why the frown, pretty lady?" Rand queried, his hand resting on her hip and his arm tightening to pull her close to his side. "It's a beautiful night, and sad, serious thoughts shouldn't mar it. I'm sorry if bringing up my dad made you look so unhappy."

"It's not that," Julie quickly assured, matching her stride to his. "I was thinking of something else." She was glad for the ocean breeze cooling her heated cheeks.

"Want to talk about it?"

Julie missed a step and would have tripped if Rand hadn't been holding her so securely. "No, nothing to talk about, actually."

What a hoot he'd have if he knew where her thoughts had been. "Prude, definitely a prude," he'd no doubt crow. Her desire was constantly warring with practical denial. That was definitely how her mind was occupied whenever she was near him, felt the warmth of his body, the hard muscles of his thighs brushing against her, smelled the scent of his flesh.

"I've talked about me long enough," Rand observed. "Now it's your turn. I know you're finishing up your doctorate in earth science and work for some institute in California. What kind of work do you do?"

She skimmed over her studies in geochemistry and briefly described her work, striving to explain it in lay terms. Suddenly she felt self-conscious and defensive. Studying volcanic rock, hydrothermal activity and reports of fissures in the ocean floor seemed such dry, impersonal pursuits when compared to the things Rand was doing. Even though her work might lead to important discoveries of new energy and mineral resources, it made dull conversation for someone outside the field. It had been her experience that people generally showed greater interest in the social sciences or health-care fields—things more closely related to human beings and hence their own lives.

"Fascinating," Rand commented with genuine enthusiasm when she finished. "Almost like the space program. Seeking brave new worlds and so on but going into the earth rather than beyond it. Right?"

"Something like that," Julie answered, surprised and pleased with his interest.

"What prompted your fascination with the earth's interior?"

"The legend of Pele, the Polynesian goddess of volcanic fire, of all things," Julie stated, grateful to add a human touch. Pele wasn't exactly human, but at least she had taken on a human shape and in her own way had displayed human strengths and weaknesses.

"Tell me about this goddess of volcanic fire," he requested against the top of her head. They were at the end of the wharf, looking out toward the *Carthaginian II*, a replica of a whaling ship riding peacefully in the harbor. Standing behind her, Rand wrapped both arms lightly around her waist and pulled her against the warmth of his body when she shivered in the night breeze.

Snuggling comfortably against him, Julie related the legend. "Pele makes her home inside an active volcano. However, sometimes she assumes human form and leaves her fiery dwelling. Once, wandering in the spirit trance, she was attracted to a nearby island by the sound of music. When she got close enough, she saw a hula ceremony taking place and joined in."

"Pele liked to party, I take it," Rand commented.

"Maybe. In another version, she was drawn by the sounds of people cheering and saw a handsome chief, Kahawali was his name, engaged in a sort of sled race down a hill. She admired his skill —"

"Did she admire the man, as well?" Rand interrupted again, beginning to think he was holding a modern-day Pele in his arms. Julie had never been able to resist a contest.

"Yes. According to the hula legend, they became lovers for three days."

"Only three days? What happens in the other legend?" he asked, hoping for an even more romantic story spanning far more than a mere three days.

"In that one, she challenged him to a race, which shocked everyone because racing the *papa hohlua* or sled was reserved for chiefs only, and the villagers were especially shocked that a woman would break the taboo."

"But that didn't bother Pele, right?" Rand asked, resting his chin against the top of Julie's head, struck again by the resemblance between the woman he held in his arms and the ancient goddess. The two had more in common than an obsession with volcanoes. As a girl, Julie had been all for the equality of sexes, furious whenever he'd tried to exclude her from anything he had thought was a strictly male pastime. "Did she win?"

"No, and it infuriated her so much she turned into lava and wiped out most of the island."

Rand couldn't prevent his laugh. "Worst example of a sore loser I've ever heard," he muttered, then quickly asked, "What happened to the handsome chief?"

"He escaped to another island, leaving his wife and children behind to perish in the inferno," Julie supplied.

"The cad. I like the hula version better."

"It was good while it lasted, at least," Julie said wistfully, sorry to put a damper on the romantic story but compelled to reveal the rest. "In the end, the chief fell in love with Pele's sister, Ha'iaka, and spent the rest of his days living happily on another island with her."

"Must have been a mere youth and didn't realize what he had with Pele."

Julie turned in Rand's arms and looked up into his face. The way he'd made the statement and the way he was looking at her, so seriously and warmly, made her think he was comparing the ancient lovers to themselves. "You think so?" she asked softly, drawn closer by the enticing amber clusters in Rand's eyes.

"I know so," he said huskily and lowered his lips to hers.

In Julie's estimation, Pele's lava could not have been any more fiery or consuming than the rush of desire that swept through her at the very first touch of Rand's lips. Trembling, she smoothed her hands up his chest, feeling the rapid beat of his heart beneath her palm. All the more exciting was the realization that Rand was as affected by their embrace as she.

She welcomed the invasion of his tongue. Her mouth burned with the fire of his sweeping conquest and her body quivered and warmed in response. Rising slightly, she returned his kiss with equal fervor. She pressed her soft curves along his lean length, letting him know how much she wanted this and more.

"Ah, Julie," Rand sighed against her lips. Pushing her head to his shoulder, he held her securely with one arm and brushed his other hand down the silken length of her blond hair.

"Lucky we're on a very public wharf or I'd have broken your rules," he murmured, leaning his forehead against hers.

"My rules?" Julie stepped as far away from him as the circle of his arms would allow. She stared up, her eyes wide and limpid, her lips soft and lightly rouged from his kiss.

"Don't look at me like that," Rand said huskily. "You know perfectly well what rules."

He tapped the tip of her nose. "All those rules that you think are necessary to keep our relationship on a proper progression."

He dropped his arms and released her. Catching her hand, he started along the wharf. "Let's walk or I'll forget where we are and lose my head. Not only would I shock a few of these people, but I'd break your rule against public displays. You really don't play fair, you know."

"I wasn't aware we were playing a game," Julie retorted, stung by his accusation and suddenly pain-

fully aware of the number of people sharing the
wharf.

Rand stopped walking and faced her. With his
hands resting lightly on her shoulders, he asked,
"Hasn't there always been some kind of contest between us? This time I'm not going to land flat on my
back, staring up at the sky."

"What are you talking about?"

"I'm saying I won't play Charlie Brown to your
Lucy. You challenge me to play, set up the rules, then
snatch the ball away at the last minute."

Seeing the confusion still plain on her face, Rand
drawled huskily, "Like right now. Do you have any
idea what your kisses are doing to me?"

He ignored her stunned expression and went on
with his accusations. "You're not wearing anything
besides a pair of panties beneath this tube of material you call a dress."

He slipped one finger beneath her floral necklace,
trailed downward, then curled it under the elasti-
cized top edge of her bodice. "One small tug and I'd
have you bared to the waist. Two more elementary
maneuvers and every inch of your perfumed, silky
skin would be available for me to see, to touch, to
taste. And then, when all I could think about was
sinking my body into yours, you'd call a halt, telling me we don't know each other well enough, yet."
He pulled slightly on the elastic and let it snap back
into place.

"You make me sound like a tease."

Shoving his hands in his pockets, Rand rocked
backward on his heels. He let his breath out slowly
and looked beyond her shoulder to the gentle swells

in the harbor. "Not exactly. You just like to stack the deck and call all the shots."

He turned his gaze back to Julie, probing beyond the protective facade he instinctively knew she'd thrown up. "You've always been that way. It used to drive me crazy. Now I consider it part of your charm," he revealed. "Funny how you look at things differently when you grow up."

"Yeah," Julie agreed without enthusiasm, her heated senses effectively chilled by his remarks. "Funnier still is how you seem to know me so well, and I'm beginning to wonder if I ever knew you at all."

With a self-derisive shrug she turned and started walking back along the wharf. Rand fell easily in step alongside her. "I must have been a very shallow kid," she remarked.

Rand caught her hand and gave it a slight squeeze. "Don't be so hard on yourself. I wasn't easy to know. I lived with me and didn't know me. Only two people knew me."

"Your parents?"

"Until dad died, that was true. Then your dad stepped right in and became the best friend a kid could ever have."

"My dad!"

They'd reached the car and Julie waited impatiently for an explanation as Rand silently unlocked it and guided her inside. When he'd taken his place behind the wheel, she asked, "Is that who you were referring to when you mentioned someone really setting you straight?"

Rand nodded in affirmation and turned the key in the ignition. "We never did get around to that, did we?'' he asked needlessly. "Will has a lot of patience and helped me let down all my angry barriers. He's a great listener. Doesn't say much but when he does, he speaks volumes."

Julie found herself chuckling, thinking of her quiet but very wise father. "That he does. He used to level me with only a word or two."

"You don't hold an exclusive franchise on that," Rand informed. "He managed to do that with me more than once. I owe him a lot. I can never repay him for all he's done."

"You're his best friend's son, Rand," Julie stated, turning as far toward Rand as her safety belt would allow. "He'd never expect anything in return. In a way, your work with children could be considered a repayment. You're reaching out to somebody who needs you, just like he did."

Rand slowed the car and turned toward her. "I hadn't thought of it like that, Julie. Maybe you're right." He grinned. "Then, you usually are."

"Not always, Rand. Not always," Julie returned quietly. "I've made a lot of mistakes. I'm as human as the next person."

Rand was forced to turn his attention back to the road. "So you are," he confirmed philosophically.

He didn't seem inclined to pursue their conversation further, and Julie settled back against the seat, needing some time to sort out her own thoughts. This part of Rand's life came as a revelation to her. She had never suspected that his grief had run so deep nor that her father had been the one to console him. How much more was there in his background that she didn't know about?

Julie had no idea what was going through Rand's mind, but he'd certainly given her lots to think about. Her father had never mentioned his close relationship with Rand, but then Willard Stites was a very quiet, unassuming person. He'd never expect any praise for helping someone. He did things for his own satisfaction.

The highway edged the shore and the soughing of the breeze through the roadside foliage should have been relaxing. A blend of scents no master perfumer could possibly create wafted through the open windows of the car and came up from the flowers draped against her skin. The mixture of fragrances should have hypnotized Julie. Instead, her mind was focused inward upon herself. How well did she know herself, or for that matter anyone else?

Had she become so obsessed with the earth's inner secrets that she'd neglected to delve beneath the surface of the people around her? It wasn't that she didn't like people. She did and hoped that her research would benefit mankind, but what of individuals? She'd not allowed herself the time to truly nurture either close friendships or intimate relationships. Unintentionally she'd kept people at arm's length. Her interests and life-style were so narrow when compared with Rand's.

Rand's job was as worthwhile as her own, and yet he still found time to extend himself even further. His work with children, his success as a teacher, proved that he was more open and generous than she was. Warmhearted and charming, he no doubt enjoyed a wide circle of friends. She didn't even want to speculate about how many of his friends were women or how close those particular friendships were.

Devoted to her work, she'd thought she was like her father but realized that wasn't true at all. Like Rand, her father had unselfishly extended himself to others. Julie knew that her parents had a strong love based on an even stronger friendship, but they still had room in their lives for their child and a myriad of friends and acquaintances. Professor Stites's office and home had always been open to his students, and often their visits had nothing to do with course work.

"Will you tell me more about you and dad?" Julie asked.

"He used to drive down to Kentucky every so often and visit me at school," Rand revealed, a gleam of humor in his dark eyes. "We'd walk, I'd talk and he'd listen. I guess, most of all, he let me know he cared and was there if I ever needed him."

"I never knew he visited you," Julie stated, surprised that she hadn't been aware of Rand's relationship with her father. Still, it made perfectly good sense. Her parents had always liked Rand, treated him like a memeber of the family. It would have been perfectly natural for Rand to have turned to Will once his own father had died.

"Do you still see him?" Julie asked, though she thought she already knew his answer. Rand would have kept up such a close relationship while she tended to set such relationships on shelves where they collected dust.

"Whenever I'm back in Granville. We've shared some good times. Don't get me wrong, I wasn't estranged from my mother or anything like that," Rand quickly supplied.

"Whenever I was feeling sorry for myself, though, thought my mother had washed her hands of me, your dad managed to get a few home truths through my thick skull," Rand disclosed this without his usual humor. "He convinced me that my mother knew best. She understood me well enough to know that I needed a strong and constant male influence. The way things were going, she thought military school was better than reform school."

"Now who's being hard on himself?" Julie teased, lightening the tone of the conversation as much for herself as for Rand. She needed no more revelations to point out how empty her life had become. Having arrived at that conclusion, she was ready to take the first step toward change. "I don't think you were quite that bad."

"Thanks for the vote of confidence, but I think your memory's gone soft," Rand returned with a chuckle. "You thought I was that bad. Come on, admit it."

"Well. . ." Julie hedged, "maybe I did get mad sometimes. There were times you made my life miserable, but you never did anything destructive or malicious."

"Not destructive?"

"You really didn't mean to set fire to your garage and the neighbors', did you?" Julie queried, setting her self-condemnation completely aside with a gurgle of laughter as she remembered the fiasco.

Rand chuckled as he parked the car. Turning toward her, he remarked, "It wasn't exactly an accident, but it wasn't my intent, either."

"Oh, yeah?" Julie challenged, smiling warmly, unconsciously leaning toward him, her gaze held by his.

"Then again, three-alarm fires can be pretty exciting," he drawled huskily, leaning across the seat. His fingertips played lightly along her shoulder.

"Mmm," Julie mused, her senses heated by his touch, more relieved than she cared to think that his interest in her hadn't been extinguished by three days of cold. "You still like setting fires?" she asked coyly, moving closer.

"They have their uses." Taking the advantage she'd given, he pressed his lips to her temple, nuzzling the pulse that throbbed there.

He nibbled a line down her cheek and Julie arched her neck, inviting his lips to explore her throat. He was lighting tiny fires with each touch of his lips, and Julie had no intention of putting them out—not this time. All evening she'd wanted to stoke life back into his desire for her.

He was right. She hadn't played fair. She'd used every bit of ammunition she could gather to bring about this end.

"Let's go inside and set one together," Julie suggested boldly, fervently hoping he wouldn't exact revenge for that bitter argument and turn the tables on her. There was absolutely nothing wrong with his lovemaking technique. When he raised his head and gave her a questioning look, she curved her palm to his jaw and smiled, concentrating everything she was feeling in that smile.

Rand turned his lips into her palm and cautioned, "It may blaze out of control."

"Probably, but I don't plan on calling any firemen."

7

THEY WERE BARELY INSIDE THE DOOR before Julie was in Rand's arms. Slanting his mouth over hers, Rand kissed her with a hunger that erased any doubts Julie had had that his desire for her had dwindled. No less was her thirst for him and she wrapped her arms around his neck, answering the demands of his firm, moist mouth.

Taking her with him, Rand leaned backward against the door to close it. Their kiss didn't end with the movement, but deepened as he crushed her to him. With one arm around her shoulders, he held her firmly. His other hand roamed down her back, hesitated at her waist, then smoothed over her hips.

The kiss went on and on as both sought to appease their craving, giving and taking all they could absorb. Their hands moved urgently over each other's bodies, as if to ensure themselves that this was happening, that neither would vaporize if they reached out to fully capture the solidity of the other.

Julie clutched at Rand's shoulders, then ran her palms along the strong, muscled column of his neck. Her fingers pushed into the warm, curling hair at his nape and upward until she cradled the back of his head in her palms. Her body melded into his until her breasts were flat against his chest and her belly fit snugly against his.

Wrapping his hand in the swathe of her hair, Rand tugged, gently tilting Julie's head back, deepening his kiss. Being exactly where she wanted to be, Julie reveled in this tender imprisonment. His hands roamed over her, sculpting her curves with his fingers and palms. He emitted an involuntary moan when her soft warmth pushed against his hardened groin.

"Your place or mine?" Rand asked shakily, setting her away from him.

"Mine. The bed's bigger."

"And I plan to make use of every inch of it," Rand remarked as he followed her down the hall.

Julie's trembling limbs weakened even more in response to his words. With all her heart she wanted the unrestricted passion he was promising. She wanted to lie in his arms, their bodies interwined, making love over and over again.

And making love it would be, Julie realized. The need she had for him, to share her body with him and enjoy his went far beyond the desire for the physical pleasures they would give each other. Tonight they would forge the most intimate bond possible between two human beings.

Once inside her room, Rand switched on the bedside lamp. "I've dreamed of having you for so long. I want to see you."

"Three days isn't that long," Julie teased in a whisper, but she knew what he meant. Every minute of those days had seemed like a century.

"It goes back longer than that," Rand confessed in a barely audible voice. He tugged gently on the lei, lowering his head as he brought her to him. He kissed her softly, tenderly, then slowly pulled the flowered necklace over her head and tossed it onto a pillow.

Seeing the tremor in his hand as he slipped his fingers beneath the shirred elastic of her dress filled her with joy. He wanted her just as badly as she wanted him. She lifted her chin, her luminous blue eyes searching for the magnetic gold of his.

For several moments they just stood there, gazes locked. Without words, without touch, promises were exchanged and fears quenched. Neither was aware of the significance in the action when simultaneously, each brought their hands to the other. All they wanted to do was seek out the treasures freely offered, gather in each new and wonderful sensation they both needed so much.

As he had predicted, it took only one elementary maneuver for Rand to bare her to the waist. Julie proved equally adept when stripping him down to his trousers. Bathed in the light from the bedside lamp, they helped each other out of the rest of their clothing until both of them stood naked. Faced with the beauty of each other's bodies, neither moved.

"Not even a goddess could compare with you, Julie," Rand whispered reverently as his hands came up to cup her full breasts. "I've dreamed of you so often, and now you're here."

Her back arched as he lowered his head to the succulent points beckoning to his lips. He caught one nipple between his teeth and caressed it with his tongue as his fingers adored the surrounding flesh. When both breasts had received equal attention, he knelt, his hands curving around her buttocks as he pressed kisses along the smooth skin of her stomach.

"Oh, Rand," she breathed in exquisite agony, chills of pleasure overcoming her. Her legs went weak, but before they gave way completely he was there to lift her into his arms. He laid her down on the bed but didn't join her until he'd spread her hair on the pillow and placed the lei like a crown of flowers upon the silken mass.

"How beautiful you look, lying there waiting for me." He lay down beside her, his weight dipping the bed so that her body slid across the sheets to meet his. "Never more beautiful," he murmured as he clasped the sides of her chin with his fingers and searched her face. "I'll make you glad you let me love you."

Love you. The words upheld the promise he was making to her with his eyes. Though she feared what he felt for her tonight might not last forever, she had never been more certain of her own feelings. She loved him and always would. "I'm already glad, Rand. There's nothing I've ever wanted more."

Rand's mouth hovered above hers, then he claimed her softly parted lips. At the warm probing of his tongue, a liquid warmth gathered and spun through Julie's limbs. His touch upon her skin was familiar yet excitingly new. Though her mind had stored the knowledge and experience of his love-making, her body found each kiss, each caress an unexpected revelation.

Julie could not wait to explore the entire length of his naked body. Her fingers began a tantalizing journey down the sleek masculine lines of his torso. With every feathery stroke, the sinew rippled and shifted beneath her fingertips. When her palm slid over the taut flesh below his navel, she felt his muscles contract. When her fingers slid lower, he groaned and grasped her hand.

"Not yet," he moaned thickly. "I'll be too far ahead of you."

Keeping her hands firmly trapped, Rand continued his own exploration. He savored her soft skin with his mouth and memorized the silky, velvet texture of her. Drawing out each second of feeling, he accompanied his heated touch with the all-encompassing devotion of his eyes.

Rand wanted to trace his mouth over each delectable, totally kissable, inch of her. The island sun had brushed her skin with gold except for the three creamy-white triangles that had been covered by her miniscule bikini. Each one of those highlighted patches beckoned to him.

His breath stopped as he placed his open mouth over the rosy bud that flowered between his lips. He heard her gasp as he tormented her vulnerable nipple and increased the pressure of his hand between her thighs. When he finally spread the petals of her femininity, she writhed beneath him but opened herself for more of his claiming strokes.

Julie moaned, spreading her thighs to accommodate his big body. The urgency he felt pulsed within her, too, and she cried out for him to take her. Arching her back as he probed deeper, she knew she could take no more and wanted him with her when the driving dance of passion reached its peak.

"Please, Rand," she begged. Gratified by the thrusting weight of him as he crushed her into the mattress, Julie's hands freed themselves and clutched frantically around his middle.

Rand filled her, surged inside her with throbbing need. When she had taken all of him within herself, she felt him pause. Startled, she opened her eyes. "Rand?"

"Look at me, Julie," he murmured huskily. "Let this be a total sharing." The gold in his eyes shimmered with a heat that could only be quenched by the sea-blue depths of hers. Watching the wondrous expression reflected in those cool pools, he moved slowly within her.

They melted into each other, absorbed each nuance of pleasure, then retreated to prepare for the next flaming surge. The pressure built and built as if it came from the bottomless energy of the earth. Together they flowed with concentric heat, spiraling toward release. Finally their bodies blended in molten fusion, then exploded in glorious volcanic passion.

When it was over they rocked toward the languorous aftermath that awaited them. Rand was first to rise from the blissful pool of sensation that had buoyed their quaking bodies. His expression was slightly stunned, his lips were dark with the brand of her kisses, and his eyes were fascinated by the similar markings on her. Two large blue-green mirrors reflected his face, her lips were moist with his taste, her breasts flushed from his possession.

"Oh, Julie." He took her with him as he rolled onto his side and, cradling her head upon his shoulder, he stroked her hair. "We're so good together. Let's stay this way forever."

Julie was delighted with his request. She would have gladly spent the rest of her life in his arms, but was afraid to trust that his words were inspired by more than the insurmountable passion they'd just shared. Not daring to reveal her need for commitment, she strove for a light tone. "That might be fun, but not too practical. Eventually we'd waste away to bare bones."

Rand chuckled. "But what a way to go." He shifted to his back and pulled her over him.

She felt the hard probe of his renewed desire surge hotly between her thighs, and at her astonished expression he leered at her. "You vanquish and restore me. I was only a mere mortal, but you, my goddess of fire, have elevated me to a new height of being."

Julie couldn't help but laugh, well aware that the rise in his being was not spiritual in nature. "Aren't you afraid you'll be consumed by my eternal fire?"

"If this goes on eternally, I will only rejoice," he growled, a triumphant quirk on his lips as his inquisitive fingers discovered her readiness and his body took advantage of her receptive welcome.

JULIE AWOKE to find herself alone in bed for the first time in two days. Her fingers brushed the indentations on the pillow beside her and she felt a twinge of regret when she found the linen cold. Last night she'd been so tired after forty-eight hours of near continuous activity that Rand's sensuous invitation had been met with a helpless yawn.

He had the stamina of six men and had dragged her from one end of Maui to the other, saying he didn't want to miss a single tourist attraction. They'd traded their sedans for a Jeep and had driven miles and miles of trails that would have been virtually impassable without four-wheel drive. They'd hiked obscure paths through flower-strewn wilderness in order to swim in hidden lagoons.

In two days they had made love beneath a sparkling waterfall, on a deserted beach under a brilliant sun and within a silent grotto created by the concealing tropical rain forest. Somehow Rand had managed to throw all her caution to the wind each time his eyes lit up with that look she knew meant he wanted her immediately. She had never felt so spontaneous, so alive.

Rand seemed to thrive on the rigorous sight-seeing schedule he set for their days and was equally energetic in bed at night. Last night when Julie had finally succumbed to exhaustion, she had staggered into bed and fallen instantly asleep, oblivious to the arms that held her and the warm press of the hard masculine body that normally aroused her.

They'd spent the previous day on a trip to Haleakala, the House of the Sun. It had taken two and a half hours to reach the summit for they'd stopped at each observatory along the way. They'd been told to wear warm clothing for, at more than ten thousand feet in altitude, the top of the mountain was downright chilly.

Julie's lips moved upward in a smile as she recalled the island legend concerning the demigod Maui and the sun. When their tour guide had told the story of how Maui had ascended Haleakala, determined to set a lower speed limit for the sun's trip across the sky, she had likened the sun's compulsive haste to the momentum Rand had set for their excursions around the island. Laughingly, she had warned him that she might use Maui's methods to force Rand to slow down.

According to the ancient story, as the sun had risen from its house, Maui had taken careful aim and lassoed the hot beast by its genitals, not releasing him until he had promised to proceed more slowly in the future. The sun had, of course, capitulated, and the whole world had benefited from Maui's imposed daylight saving time. Upon hearing Julie's threat, Rand had winced but then had whispered such an indecent suggestion in her ear that she'd had trouble concentrating on their guide's subsequent tales of Maui's trickster ways.

That evening they'd exchanged their warm clothes for cooler island attire and driven over to the Royal Lahaina Hotel. They'd danced to a disco beat in the Foxy Lady then braved a mob of gyrating islanders rocking to the music at the Wet Noodle. By the time they'd gotten back to their villa, Julie's eyes had been out of focus and her legs unable to carry her another step. She'd fallen asleep to the sound of Rand's entreaty, "Come on Julie, the night's still young. Let's go for a moonlight swim."

She didn't know or care if Rand had gone down to the beach. This morning, however, she felt refreshed and would have liked to have awakened to find him beside her. Now that she was in the mood for more adventure, her imaginative social director was nowhere in sight. She stretched her arms over her head and let out a disappointed sigh. It looked like she was going to have to leave the luxurious comfort of the king-size bed and go in search of him.

One bare limb was seeking the plush carpeting on the floor when she heard what could only be described as raucous croaking. She recognized the Hawaiian Wedding Song only by the lyrics, for the melody was being unmercifully butchered. Julie's brows shot up as the off-key crooner appeared in the threshold of the sliding glass doors.

As much as she tried not to grimace over the inhuman sounds, she tried harder not to smile in vast appreciation of his appearance. Rand wore nothing but a knee-length grass skirt and a bright red hibiscus lei. With each movement of the hula, the dried reeds gave her a tantalizing glimpse of powerful male thighs and sleek flanks.

Rand warbled loudly, "Promise me that you will leave me never..." waving his arms in the traditional movements of the dance.

Completely entranced, ignoring the punishment he was delivering to her eardrums, Julie leaned back against the pillows to enjoy the show. Don Ho he was not, but he had a body that made one forget that his voice came from someplace other than heaven. What's more, the devil himself would have been proud of the suggestion in Rand's lewd gyrations. Blunt-tipped fingers beckoned to her, telling an X-rated story, and each gesture was matched by the titillating movements of tight buttocks and lean hips.

As the shocking routine progressed, Julie found it more and more difficult to breathe. No wonder the early missionaries had tried to suppress this dance. The message Rand conveyed with each undulating motion of his lower body was sinfully erotic. Rand's hula attempt was hardly the classic dance of religious ritual, but a modern version of fast-hipped bump and grind.

Eventually she covered her heated cheeks with her hands and pleaded, "Stop. Stop. I can't take anymore."

"But I've got so much more to show you, my *nani wahine*," Rand assured wickedly. "I come to worship at your feet, my goddess of fire. I dance the hula for you alone, seeking your favor. I might not be of these islands, but surely I can tempt you with the *nui nani* of my heart."

"Your heart isn't the only big, beautiful thing about you, you handsome *malihine*," Julie declared breathlessly, opening her arms to him.

Rand launched himself toward the bed and the woman who waited for him. "I won't be a stranger to you long," he promised with a feral show of white teeth. "Last night I feared I had lost your interest and had to do something to regain it."

"You've regained it, all right." Julie giggled.

Fingers clasped in the blond tangles of her hair, Rand positioned her head to receive his kiss. Julie reacted to the naked male desire in him as if to a potent drug. As his mouth closed hot and passionately demanding over hers, she stroked his smoothly muscled back with the tips of her nails.

With a low sound of masculine need and triumph, Rand levered himself up from her and demanded, "Get rid of that sheet."

Julie was more than happy to comply with his rough order. Since she was naked beneath the light cover, she thought it only fair that he remove the scratchy garment that encircled his loins. He had trouble untying it and finally, in frustration, he yanked at the woven girdle. The cord broke and a shower of raffia descended on Julie and the bed.

Oblivious to the debris scattered over his willing conquest, he lowered himself over her and took her mouth again. Julie squirmed beneath him, not only because of the overwhelming need she felt but because of the irritating fibers from his skirt that scratched her skin. Finally Rand became aware of her discomfort and swiftly brushed the dried reeds away.

Then she felt nothing but Rand and the fragile hibiscus blossoms crushed between them. Julie cried out softly, embracing Rand tightly as she heard his quick labored breaths merge with her own. He murmured her name as he gave up control of his body and lost himself within her.

Neither of them moved as the phone on the bedside table began ringing. Julie felt as if her arms and legs were made of a weighted liquid, and she couldn't muster the strength to lift the receiver. Rand groaned and reluctantly raised his head from between her breasts. He reached for the phone but was not yet willing to separate himself from Julie.

"Mom?" Rand pronounced in an astonished rasp. A dull red flush came up on his cheeks as he hurriedly added, "Of course I'm not angry with you anymore. I just...wasn't expecting your call."

He tried to escape the silken legs wrapped around his thighs, but Julie tightened her grasp. Having any kind of advantage over him came so rarely that she couldn't resist the temptation. As he mumbled something indecipherable into the phone, she trailed one fingertip down his spine, adding to his discomfort. Her action was rewarded by a furious glare and a desperate shaking of his head.

"No, I'm not sick," he gruffly assured his mother. "There's nothing wrong with my voice." He tried to roll away from his smiling captor, but she refused to let him go.

"That's a matter of opinion," Julie teased in a low whisper against his throat, thinking of his recent serenade. She increased his torture, lifting her head and pressing her moist mouth to his chest. She flicked her tongue across a flat nipple, stifling a laugh when Rand arched his spine, frantically trying to squirm away.

"What?" Rand asked, swallowing the obstruction in his throat. "No, you're not interfering, mom. Of course not. That's right, Julie and I are getting along a lot better."

Grabbing for the hand that was snaking below his waist, Rand swore under his breath, "Dammit, Julie. Stop that." He gave Julie a killing look but his attention immediately reverted back to the questioning voice on the phone. "No, I didn't say that. There must be interference on the line. I'm having a lot of trouble hearing you, too."

Julie quickly retracted her free hand from his taut buttocks when she noticed the sudden look of relief and satisfaction that came over his face. She silently mouthed, "No, no, no," when she heard him say, "Her mom wants to talk to her? Sure, I'll call her to the phone."

Muffling the receiver against his chest, Rand called loudly through a huge smile, "Julie! Your mom's on the phone."

"Heh, heh, heh." He chuckled evilly into Julie's ear. "Your turn." He pressed the receiver into her hand.

Placing her hand over the mouthpiece, Julie whispered, "I can't talk to her like this. Get off me!"

Smirking, Rand molded one of her breasts in his hand. "I've tried, but a certain party is unwilling to break our connection."

"Well, she is now," Julie hissed, sucking in her breath as Rand rolled one nipple between his thumb and forefinger.

Rand pointed to the phone. "Better not keep your mom waiting. This is long-distance."

Julie's body was one big blush when Rand finally relented and rolled away. Plucking the receiver from her, he informed his mother that Julie had evidently stepped outside but that he would have her call Angela a little later in the day. He hung up the phone, then gathered Julie back into his arms.

"You're gonna pay now, Stilts," he forewarned darkly.

It was almost two hours later before Julie was allowed to make the overseas call to her mother. Just as Rand had done with his mother, she assured her own that she and Rand were enjoying their vacation and had agreed to share the villa amicably.

Unfortunately the conversation reminded Julie of her initial anger with their mothers' matchmaking. Neither she nor Rand had admitted to their respective parents that they were sharing much, much more than living space. Julie felt it would be handing them a triumph and provoking her own mother to ask questions that Julie had no intention of answering. She was sure the calls from Ohio would only become more frequent. Julie didn't know about Rand, but she wasn't about to provide the romantic material for the next Angel Sylver book.

It was far too soon to admit that Angela and Sylvia may have done them a favor. Feeling insulted that their parents had taken matters into their own hands and pulled such a maneuver with their adult children, Julie needed to exact a little revenge. It would do those two romantics good to stew in their own juices a little while longer.

Foremost in her mind, however, was Julie's own insecurity—the things not said between her and Rand. If things didn't work out between them, Julie prayed Angela and Sylvia would never find out what had happened here at the villa. If her expectations for a more lasting relationship with Rand came to nothing, she'd keep the disappointment to herself. For the time being, she intended to take each day as it came. Privately she would savor the glory of this newfound relationship and, privately, she would mourn its passing.

I'M SURPRISED you don't have one of these, Rand," Julie commented as she flipped on her computer. "Surely a university as large as Columbia has been using them for years."

Leaning over her shoulder, Rand watched Julie type the necessary codes to boost in the appropriate program. "They have been, but I haven't used one of these little portable jobs."

"This model isn't all that expensive and would probably be worth the investment to you, personally," Julie informed him, reaching for her box of diskettes and loading one in a disk drive. "You must write as much as my dad does. After our mothers bought computers for their work, mom convinced my dad he ought to give it a try."

Julie twisted in her chair and grinned at Rand. "Once dad got the hang of it, he and mom nearly came to blows over computer time and dad had to go out and buy his own. He bought a portable similar to this one, and it's compatible with mom's and her printer. Now he lets her borrow his when she and Sylvia are traveling for research or promotion."

"Maybe I'll look into it when I get back," Rand allowed, fascinated as he watched Julie demonstrate moving words and paragraphs. "Thanks for the quick lesson in word processing. You're a good teacher," he complimented, dropping a kiss on her bare shoulder. "If you ever got tired of studying volcanoes, you could land a job with some university. You've got a real easy way of getting information across."

"I've got a willing and able pupil," Julie countered, smiling.

"I'll confess to some computer knowledge," Rand admitted with a slightly sheepish grin. Sobering he added, "But seriously, think about what I said. If for some reason you want to leave the research end, you'd be a natural in the classroom."

The way his eyes seemed to be probing hers made Julie uneasy. It was as if he was searching for an answer from her and Julie wished she knew the question. Suddenly his eyes took on their familiar mischievous gleam.

"You'd certainly have the interest of all your male students. I'm willing to place a sizable bet that your class would be very popular." At her frown, he sobered again. "Show me how the data base works."

Julie complied and Rand's enthusiasm grew. "Professor," Julie addressed him after the short lesson, "you have definitely been hiding in your dusty ivory tower. It's time you joined the computer age. It's also time we both got a little work done."

She tried to shoo him over to his own makeshift desk, but Rand insisted he wanted to watch her work for a while. Promising to remain quiet, he stood behind her and gazed over her shoulder at the computer monitor. Julie loaded her program and began scrolling the text. "You'll be bored with this, Rand," she cautioned. "It's pretty dry stuff."

Boldly, in capital letters, a phrase leaped off the screen. "GO TO BED WITH THE MAN AND RELIEVE THIS FRUSTRATION."

"What an interesting premise you've presented, Miss Stites," Rand deemed, adopting a professorial attitude. "Perhaps you'd like my assistance in researching this theory a little more thoroughly. After all, if you want to get a doctorate, you've got to provide valid documentation. I have some credentials your board might recognize. I'd be happy to give a testimonial on your behalf."

"Oh, no." Julie sighed and dropped her face into her hands as Rand's uproarious laughter echoed in her ears. He would never let her forget this telling lapse.

"And all the time I thought you fell into my arms because you couldn't resist my winning ways, you were just gathering material to support your hypothesis. Don't you feel guilty for callously using me for your own scientific experimentation? Have you no ethics?"

Julie screwed her mouth to one side and raised one brow at him. "How long do I have to listen to this malarkey?"

"Until you tell me whether or not it worked," Rand disclosed gleefully. "Perhaps we should retire to the boudoir in order to discover if you suffer from lingering sexual frustration. I've tried to do my best, but never let it be said that Dr. Randall B. Maxwell isn't willing to go that extra mile to further the cause of science."

"I've already gathered enough proof of that," Julie assured quickly, though her body said otherwise as Rand's hands ran up underneath her T-shirt. She gasped as his lips dropped to the nape of her neck and he began nipping at the soft skin.

"Rand!" she wailed desperately, squirming in her chair. Her nipples were hard pebbles against his palms and the corresponding ache between her thighs told her how easily he could ambush her powers of concentration. "I have to work."

"I understand that. I'm helping you." His warm breath tickled her ear before he took the tender lobe between his teeth. At the same time, one large hand slipped beneath the elastic waistband of her shorts.

Breathing rapidly, Julie managed, "Aren't you ever satisfied?"

"Not so's you'd notice," he countered wolfishly.

The afternoon was spent compiling more research in Julie's quest for knowledge.

BY THE MIDDLE of their second week on the island, neither of them had accomplished more than a modicum of work. They decided to stay on an extra week but realized if they were going to get anything done, they would have to separate. Rand put in a call to the East-West Center and learned that the director, Dr. Charles Masaoka, had returned from the mainland. Delighted with his luck, Rand arranged to meet with him.

Julie placed a similar call to the U.S. geological survey office on the Big Island and set up her tour of the Hawaiian Volcano Observatory. They planned to stay away from the villa for at least three days, each promising to return there at approximately the same time. They drove to the airport at Kahului together but boarded planes headed in opposite directions.

On the flight to Hilo, Julie's thoughts were not on the magnificent volcano mountains she would soon view but the tumultuous interlude she had just shared with Rand. In one way she was glad to have a few days away from him. She was beginning to feel as if she'd been living in a dreamworld, an isolated Eden where only the two of them existed. Neither one of them had even tried to spy the serpents in their paradise—and there were serpents.

Rand had serenaded her with the Hawaiian Wedding Song, but she wondered if she would ever hear those vows for real. He'd said a lot of beautiful things when he'd made love to her, but could she count on his feelings to continue past their vacation? They lived on opposite coasts, and the problems inherent in a long-distance relationship seemed insurmountable.

Rand surely wouldn't be willing to give up his position at Columbia and move to Los Angeles. And, to be honest, Julie had to admit that if he asked her to make that kind of sacrifice, she'd have to refuse. She'd worked long and hard and was just now attaining one of her goals. Before Rand had come back into her life, she'd been exactly where she wanted to be, working closely with the best volcanologists in America. But he had taught her how to play, and she didn't know if she could live without that now.

8

THE NIGHT AIR was filled with sulfuric fumes as if ancient Pele's vaporous breath was blowing over the Big Island. The sky glowed red above the gently sloping cone of Mauna Loa, the world's tallest active volcano. After almost ten years of napping, the sleeping dragon had awakened. Fifteen miles away, Julie, along with several scientists from the Hawaiian Volcano Observatory, watched the spectacle through binoculars.

Shortly after midnight the seismographs had set off jagged warning lines—molten rock was on the move far beneath the earth's surface. Now, a short three hours later, Julie watched twin rivers of lava flow over the crater's rim. Though she'd witnessed some of Mount St. Helen's activity in 1980, it had been an entirely different kind of eruption than that which was happening here in the Pacific.

Recalling the spring she'd spent in the Cascade Mountains of the Pacific Northwest, Julie thought about the contrast in geophysics Mount St. Helens had displayed. Because of an earthquake west of the summit of the mountain, volcanologists, geologists and meteorologists were able to record a sequence of spectacular events Julie would never forget.

Early on in the observation, the north flank of the peak had begun to bulge nearly two hundred sixty

feet out of its original position. Scientists had recognized it as a warning sign, but Mount St. Helens
had selfishly kept the time, magnitude and long-
range effects of her eruption a secret. Thus, when on
a quiet morning in May yet another, larger, earthquake occurred, followed within seconds by an ex-
plosion that rivaled Vesuvius, the humans keeping
close watch were taken by surprise.

The earthquake caused numerous avalanches,
and very soon thereafter the entire north face of the
mountain separated and the slope fell in a cata-
strophic avalanche. A large blast carrying ash and
stony fragments overtook the avalanche, destroy-
ing everything in its path. Next came a pyroclastic
flow and landslide that carried remnants of the north
flank nearly twenty miles down the Toutle River
Valley, which was then buried to depths as great as
a hundred eighty feet.

A flow of pumice dammed the outlet of Spirit
Lake and a vertical column began to rise rapidly,
reaching almost two hundred feet in the air. The re-
sulting ash fall traveled as far east as central Mon-
tana and eventually circled the globe, causing hazy
skies and red sunsets. When it was all over, damage
was estimated in excess of two billion dollars, thirty-
four people were dead and thirty-two were listed as
missing.

In comparison, Mauna Loa was behaving like a
lady. True, she'd given only a few hours' warning,
but her behavior had been more predictable and not
nearly as violently destructive. Whereas Mount St.
Helens had smoldered for weeks then literally blown
her top, Mauna Loa was putting on a show of temper, quickly fused but not expected to be sizable.

An important difference between the two volcanoes, especially for Julie, was that Mauna Loa was extruding molten lava or magma from the core of the earth—the very substance Julie was most interested in studying. She couldn't have timed her visit to the observatory better.

Upon her arrival in Hilo the previous day, she'd contacted the observatory and confirmed her appointment. Thus, knowing of her presence on the island, a member of the staff had notified her of the eruption within an hour of the first warning and sent someone to pick her up at the hotel.

"What do you think, Miss Stites?" Harry Kula grinned at her from his position behind the telescope. He nodded toward the lava flow on the slope miles away. "Should we break out the gin?" His white-toothed grin was broad in his round face.

Julie stared blankly in response. "To celebrate?" she asked, puzzled.

Harry's brown eyes twinkled with merriment. "No, *haole*," he corrected with gentle patience. "To appease Pele before the old girl gets so mad she blows up the island."

Julie chuckled and joined in the joke. "Might be a good idea. She's supposed to have a taste for it. As I understand it, somebody has to throw some bottles in her path. Are you volunteering to run up there with a case of Beefeaters?" she returned with a twinkling smile of her own.

From the first moment, the staff had accepted her as a colleague. Though a volcano was erupting off in the distance and the scientists were busy recording the event, they'd managed to extend island hospitality to her. Easygoing in spite of all the confusion, they'd introduced themselves and included her in all the activities. *Haole* was the Hawaiian word for mainlander, and though they teased her, they hadn't made her seem like an outsider. Her credentials had preceded her and she was welcomed as part of the team.

"Waste of good booze," Kim White muttered disappointedly, lowering her binoculars. "Looks like she's stopped."

Those who hadn't been watching turned their binoculars back to the lava. Kim was right. The red rivers had streamed an estimated thousand feet down the cone and stopped. The group of scientists and park rangers that had gathered to watch the eruption continued to monitor a while longer. Finally all were in agreement that the lava had ceased flowing. When and if it would start again was anybody's guess.

Some of the observers were disappointed. Others were more optimistic and considered the stoppage merely temporary. It was still night, that normally blackest part in the last hours before the dawn. The observers split into three groups.

The most pessimistic chose to return to their homes and catch a few hours' sleep. Another group volunteered to continue monitoring the volcano. The last group, Julie among them, chose to move to the Volcano House, the hotel located on the very edge of the Kilauea Crater, the island's other live volcano. For the past several years, Kilauea had put on an almost monthly display, but one so mild, tourists were often able to view the activity right from the rim.

"We can probably get one of the lounges to open for us and we can at least get a cup of coffee," Harry explained. "We can still see Mauna Loa from there and enjoy the view in a lot more comfort."

Julie and three young members of the U.S. geological survey team piled into Harry's Land Rover. The trip down the rugged trail that wound through the lush Waiakea Forest was jarring, but Julie's spirits remained undaunted. The others, though used to frequent eruptions at Kilauea, were not much less excited. Whereas Kilauea smoldered, sputtered and gurgled, Mauna Loa was showing far more spunk, as if she'd saved up her energy and was now releasing it.

"Awesome, just awesome," Harry repeated as he held the lobby door open for Julie and the others. Shaking his head as he cast one more look in Mauna Loa's direction before he entered the building, he remarked more to himself than the others, "Has to be seen to be believed."

Julie couldn't have agreed more. This wasn't her first trip to the Big Island, and she'd witnessed some of the lava flows from the many other craters to be found in Hawaii Volcanoes National Park. However, Mauna Loa, that lofty, regal giant, had been silent, having last erupted briefly in 1975.

Only time, possibly weeks or months, would tell just how active she would become. The sensitive instruments developed in the past decade were still incapable of providing all the answers and predictions required for accurate forewarning. Much was known, but each new discovery not only answered questions but raised more. That was the frustration of being a research scientist, it was also the challenge that kept people like Julie and the others continuing.

Passing through the lobby, Julie spied several pay telephones along one wall. Excusing herself from the others, she headed for the closest booth. For the first time since she'd been awakened with the news of the eruption, she thought of Rand.

She dialed island information and obtained the number for Rand's hotel in Honolulu. A soft smile touched her lips as she imagined him sleeping and the reasons why his slumber might be especially sound. No matter what he claimed, Rand was mortal and even his body needed to rest.

He had probably fallen into his bed in Oahu as eagerly as she had in hers, here on the Big Island. They hadn't slept much last night. Their lovemaking had taken on a special intensity knowing they would be separated for several days and nights.

Guiltily she dialed his hotel and waited while the night clerk rang his room. She was sorry to disturb him, but she wasn't sure when she'd get another chance to call him. Anticipating a sleepy answer, Julie leaned against the booth and imagined how Rand would look.

His hair would be tousled and falling across his forehead. His eyes would be soft and his body warm and. . .nude. She gulped and nearly dropped the receiver.

She didn't think he owned a pair of pajamas—at least she hadn't seen any. But then, he hadn't seen any of the nightgowns she'd brought with her.

As she'd expected, Rand's answer was muffled and barely intelligible. "Rand. It's me, Julie," she supplied, warmed by the mere sound of his breathing.

Before he could question her reason for calling so early in the morning, she babbled. "The most wonderful thing has happened. Mauna Loa has erupted and I got to see it. Red hot lava's pouring over her rim and it's the chance of a lifetime. I don't know when I'll be able to call you again or even when I'll get back to Maui."

Suddenly sounding fully awake, Rand demanded, "An eruption? A full-fledged eruption? Where are you?"

"I'm with some others at the Volcano House," she told him, oblivious to the worry in his tone as she explained exactly what the Volcano House was and where it was located.

"Is that safe?" he questioned, alarm in his voice. "How do you know this one won't go off?"

"It's safe," she assured. "The two haven't erupted at the same time for more than a century. Quit worrying, I only called to let you know what's happening and why I might be unavailable if you tried to call me at my hotel in Hilo."

"Julie..." he pronounced her name warningly.

"I can't talk any longer, Rand," Julie inserted, mildly irritated by his parental tone. It was the last thing she wanted from him. Hadn't she had enough meddling from parents in the past two weeks?

"I've got to call the Institute and let them know I'm here. They may be sending someone over and I may have to make some arrangements. Go back to sleep, I'll call when I get a chance." She hung up before he could say anything more.

She did have people to call and spent several more minutes contacting the Carlton Institute. As she'd expected, the director, Dr. David Lloyd, was already aware of the eruption and had been receiving information since the first indication of something happening. He was delighted that she was already on the island and urged her to stay close to the progress. Vincent Parmegelli, another geologist from the Institute, had already boarded a plane for Hilo and would be arriving in a few hours.

Once her call to Dr. Lloyd was finished, Julie went to join the others in the lounge. The excitement she'd been feeling was marred by Rand's response to her news. She hadn't realized how much she had counted on his understanding, his being as thrilled about the eruption as she.

Her disappointment was a niggling pain. A small fissure had split the walls of bliss that had isolated the two of them from the realities of their separate worlds. Was this the beginning of the pain she'd anticipated as a result of becoming involved with Rand? But she wasn't just involved with him, she was in love with him. If she had felt anything less, the disappointment wouldn't have hurt so much.

As she sat down with the others and the mug of coffee that awaited her, she tried to shake off the negative feelings she'd allowed to settle over her. Surely she was overreacting. For goodness' sake, she'd awakened the man in the dead of night.

It was completely unfair of her to condemn him for his reaction. Besides, his caution merely indicated concern for her, and concern was a sign of caring, she reminded herself. *You're just looking for trouble where there is none,* she chastised.

Julie had little time to think about her personal life during the next few days. Later that first morning, a fissure opened on Mauna Loa's side spewing a curtain of lava twenty stories high and half a mile long. Eight hours later, upwelling magma split her side again. Choking clouds of sulfur dioxide filled the air and the lava began to move through the Waiakea Forest, leaving the lush vegetation in cinders.

As if jealous of the attention being paid her sister, Kilauea started spurting lava from a rift on her own flanks. Julie divided her time between the observatory's data room and the projection room. Miles of film taken from helicopters that flew over the crater needed to be studied.

"Tell me about that gorgeous man from the mainland," Kim White begged as she turned off the projector.

Julie gulped and then quickly recovered. "What gorgeous man?"

"'What gorgeous man,' she evades," Kim parodied. "Vince Parmegelli. Are you blind or protecting your own property?"

"He's not my property," Julie quickly supplied.

"Is he married?"

"Nope." Julie put the film away in a can and labeled it for shipment to L.A.

On their way out of the room, Julie tried to keep a frown from her face. It had been obvious from the moment Kim had been introduced to Vince that she was attracted to him. Ensnared by the fatal Parmegelli charm, Julie mused. She'd seen it happen nearly every time a woman anywhere between puberty and ninety came in contact with the man.

Julie herself couldn't claim to have always been immune to his old-world charm and disgracefully long, black eyelashes. Vince had a way of looking at a woman that made her think that, at that moment, she was the only other person on earth. Only Julie's deep-seated determination to establish her credibility at the Carlton Institute had kept her in control of her reactions to the man.

Dr. Vincent Parmegelli, a string of impressive degrees and achievements behind his name, was also blessed with a tall, rangy body. He moved with incredible grace, had classic Roman features and could charm the birds out of the trees. He loved women and usually that affection was wholeheartedly returned. The more Julie had come to realize that, the more determined she had been not to join the numbers who swooned every time he passed by.

Julie's respect for Vince's work and the desire she had to learn from him had enabled her to keep him at arm's length. He was her colleague, sometimes her teacher and as close to a friend as either of them would allow. They were a lot alike, Julie supposed. She and Vince kept relationships very superficial, though she suspected many of his nights were not spent alone. Still, she doubted he shared his emotions nearly as easily as he shared his body.

Julie tried to think of a way to warn Kim about the man. It wasn't that he took advantage of women, he just allowed them to take advantage of him, all the while making them no promises. Once those facts were known, Julie decided Kim could make up her own mind about becoming involved with him.

The two women had become fairly close in the short time they'd known each other. Sharing monitoring shifts and makeshift sleeping and changing quarters at the observatory had forged a bond between them. Though Kim was nearly as tall as Julie, their appearances contrasted sharply. Kim's brown eyes, straight dark hair and fuller figure reflected her Polynesian ancestry. Island born and reared, Kim was more relaxed and far more open than Julie.

"So?" Kim questioned, as they walked out into the hallway. She began shoving coins into a vending machine. Not bothering to ask her preference, Kim slapped a can of lemon-lime soda in Julie's hand. "Here, drink it down and then we'll talk about the distinguished Dr. Parmegelli."

Grateful for the refreshment, Julie nearly drained the can in one long swallow. Pausing to catch her breath, she rolled the chilled can against her sweating forehead, wishing with all her heart that she was standing beneath a cold shower or maybe that enchanting, secluded waterfall she and Rand had discovered. It was hot, humid and all of Hilo was caught in the smoky lee of Mauna Loa. Julie didn't think she'd ever get the smell of sulfur out of her system.

"All right," Kim broke in impatiently. "So what gives with Dr. Gorgeous? If he's up for grabs, why aren't you after him?"

"He's just not my type, I guess." Julie shrugged, dropping down on one of the benches lining the wall and stretching her long legs out in front of her.

Vince's deep, smoldering gazes had never turned her knees to water. His polished ways hadn't made her yearn to be in his arms. His handsome face and trim body had caught her attention, certainly. She was as human as the next woman, but nothing about Vince had held her interest.

She'd needed the glitter of gold sparkling down at her from eyes that laughed more often than they smoldered. Rand had a handsome face and a gorgeous body, and he could be quite polished when he chose. But it was his open warmth, honesty and sometimes bumbling ways that most endeared him to her. She sighed, wishing he was there. If only she could snatch a few minutes with him.

"There's someone else," Kim announced. "I can see it in the faraway look in your eyes."

"Yes, there is, someone I've known for a long time," Julie disclosed, surprised at how easy the admission had been. It felt good to take a few minutes away from the hectic pace she and Kim had been maintaining for the past few days, to talk about something other than lava flows and seismograph readings.

"You love him," Kim stated matter-of-factly, sitting down beside her. "Tell me about him."

With that minimal command, Kim pulled out the story of Julie's reacquaintance with Rand. Once started, Julie revealed most of the past two weeks, editing the more intimate details but evidently saying enough for Kim to draw the right conclusions. When she finished, Julie drew a long breath, suddenly terribly embarrassed.

She'd never done anything like this before—hadn't even described much about her dates to her college roommate, a young woman she'd lived with for most of their four undergraduate years. This kind of personal disclosure was totally out of character for her. Was it the islands' influence? Kim White herself? Or was she doing an about-face in all relationships because of the sobering look she'd recently taken at herself?

"My mother should do me such a favor," Kim lamented enviously. "But you're afraid it won't last, right?"

"Right," Julie confirmed. "Even Eden didn't last forever."

"No, but Adam and Eve didn't break up when they were kicked out of Paradise." Kim lightly smacked Julie's knee as she rose from the bench. "My dear new friend. Love can be the pits or the heights. Either way, it's worth it. Take it from me, I'm an expert. I fall in and out as regularly as Kilauea erupts."

Julie smiled wearily at the pretty Hawaiian, then stood up and continued, "But think of the destruction to your emotions when it's over."

"You don't know that will happen any more than any of us know how long Mauna Loa's going to continue acting up," Kim admonished. "Would you have missed this?"

"No. Is this the volcanologist rendition of better to have loved and lost than never to have loved at all?"

"You got it, kid," Kim admitted as she fell in step beside Julie. "Now that we've solved your love life, let's get to mine. I want to know all you can tell me about Vincent Parmegelli. An Italian volcanologist. What an explosive combination."

RAND SHIFTED HIMSELF FORWARD to the edge of the chair and turned up the volume on the television. The news bulletins had continued all day, but this time the civil defense director was advising everybody in Hilo to begin preparing for an evacuation. A river of lava from Mauna Loa was traveling at half a mile an hour straight for the city. Nearby, on the flanks of Kilauea, lava spurted from a rift and it too was inexorably creeping towards the outskirts of Hilo.

As if Rand wasn't anxious enough about Julie's safety, that doomsday announcement was followed by videotape of a crew of intrepid "combat geologists" dressed in insulated jump suits and helmets, crouched beside a neon-orange river of fire. Armed with heat shields, they were taking temperature and flow readings, samples of gases and chunky lava. Although it was impossible to identify any one of them, Rand was almost beside himself with worry.

He'd credited Julie with enough sense to leave the Volcano House once Kilauea had erupted, but what if she'd volunteered to accompany that daredevil crew into the inferno? It would be just like her to jeopardize her own health for the good of science.

A few moments later, another less-than-calm sounding reporter relayed the news that one of the scientists at greatest risk was a staff member of the Carlton Institute in Los Angeles. This fearless volcanologist had ventured out to the river of melted rock in order to clock the flow so adequate notice could be given for the evacuation.

That was all Rand needed to hear. "Dammit, Julie!" he cursed the white-suited figure pictured on the screen. Surrounded by smoke, the masked idiot stood less than a yard from the flaming river, then gave a thumbs-up sign to the cameras. "Like it or not, you little fool, I'm getting you out of there."

Forgetting all about the promise he'd made to himself not to interfere in Julie's work, he switched off the television and grabbed the phone. In order to reach her, he'd have to get past the police and the blockades, show proof that he was more than an awestruck tourist who had come to witness the spectacle. He called the East-West Center and asked for Charles Masaoka.

If anyone would know how to get clearance through the security surrounding the volcanic eruption, Rand knew it would be the renowned expert in political science. The man knew everybody there was to know in the islands. Rand didn't care how many strings might have to be pulled, he was going to Hawaii. That spiteful goddess, Pele, could parade her awesome power before the world, but one Julie Ann Stites would have to watch the perilous exhibition from a safe distance. And, from Rand's point of view, that distance was at least one island away.

Unaware of the nerve-wracking time Rand had spent listening to reports of the cataclysmic events taking place on Hawaii, or that he feared she'd put herself in danger, Julie was working inside the offices of the volcano observatory, monitoring seismographic readings. All around her, newly met colleagues were busy recording some of the best messages ever sent from the underworld in the history of volcanology. Excitement fairly crackled in the air as an exhausted team of geologists returned from the site with samples of lava. Due to the successful maneuvering of two interfering but well-meaning matchmakers, Julie had postponed her trip to the observatory for a week. Because of the days she'd spent with Rand, she now happened to be in the right place at the right time to witness a dramatic double eruption. This was the first time since 1868 that Hawaii's two active volcanoes had erupted simultaneously. Many in her field worked their whole lives without getting the chance to view such a rare and intriguing episode. Even if she and Rand eventually decided to go their separate ways, she would never regret a moment of time she'd spent in the islands.

Caught up in the excitement of those around her, Julie worked nonstop for the rest of the day. There was something new to learn every minute, a score of theories that either fell by the wayside or were enhanced by each analysis that came in. Julie realized how fortunate she was to be present at such a bonanza for scientists and was reluctant to forgo her observations for even a second. Their round-the-clock watch would provide extensive data for all geophysicists and geochemists who were trying to explain the structure and chemical composition of the planet's interior.

Eventually, however, her hunger pains became acute and she was forced to take a well-deserved break. She and Vince, who had just come in from the field, went down to eat in the small cafeteria in the basement. Julie was tired, but Vince looked as if he might pass out from complete exhaustion. His brown eyes were rimmed with red, his black hair coated with ash and his handsome face streaked with soot. It looked as if the effort to chew on a bologna sandwich was almost too much for him.

"Can you keep your eyes open long enough to tell me what it was like out there?" Julie urged, once they'd taken the edge off their appetites.

"Mmm." Vince shrugged tiredly, then correctly interpreting the avid look on her face, sat up straighter in his chair. "Wouldn't care to postpone this inquisition until after I've scrubbed off a few pounds of sulfur dioxide dust, would you?"

"Not on your life," Julie intoned firmly. "You're the only eyewitness who owes me money for the gallons of coffee I've bought him. Spill your guts, Dr. Parmegelli, and you walk out of here a free man. I'll cancel all debts."

Vince exhaled a dramatic sigh of relief. "You mean I won't have to take out that second mortgage on the house? I won't have to live in fear that you'll send your henchmen out after me to break both my legs?"

"Nope." Julie grinned, then begged, "C'mon, Vince. Tell me everything you saw. How close did you get? How far down does Mauna Loa draw the magma?"

"Well, I didn't jump in the crater and go down a hundred miles or so to get my hands on the stuff," Vince teased. "But I got as close as any sane man could get."

At the exasperated look Julie shot him, he relented and relayed more pertinent details. "The samples we took strengthen the theory that shield volcanoes can draw magma from as far down as eighteen hundred miles in the earth's mantle. As far as we know, this flow is a plume of heated material that broke through from the mantle."

"Incredible," Julie breathed. "I wish they'd let me go out there. Just think, you've stood right next to a flow of molten rock that might have come up from the very core of the earth."

"I wasn't thinking much about that when I was out there," Vince said before chugging down the last of his soft drink. "I was scared silly. It was like stepping into the pages of Dante's Inferno." A portion of the awe he'd experienced was reflected in his eyes as he quoted the Italian poet, "All hope abandon, ye who enter here."

Not once had Julie attached a sense of evil to anything she'd learned in her studies. Far below the earth's surface was a place composed of molten liquid. This material was in all likelihood much hotter than the 2,200 degrees Fahrenheit of the lava flowing from the nearby volcanoes, but she'd never related that hellish heat to devilish forces. To her, the earth held a myriad of wonderful secrets and mankind could only benefit from each one that was uncovered.

"I doubt I would have had that feeling," she announced truthfully. "We're so lucky to have this tiny glimpse at a great unknown. We've got the chance to study material that springs from a place where no man has ever been. Unlike astronauts, we can't get in a space capsule and explore. H.G. Wells took us on a journey to the center of the earth, but that was only in his imagination. This is for real."

Once started, she got carried away on a tide of idealistic enthusiasm. "I can think of few endeavours more worthwhile than unlocking the complex mysteries that have fascinated mankind for ages."

"Then perhaps you wouldn't mind unlocking a very simple mystery for me," a harsh male voice interrupted from behind her.

Julie swiveled around in her chair, eyes going wide at the sight of a very irate-looking Rand Maxwell staring down at her. His normally relaxed features appeared to be etched in stone, his eyes reflecting a maelstrom of fury. The amber flashes blazing out of those dark orbs reminded Julie of the violent explosions she'd so recently viewed from the observatory.

"Rand? Why are you here? Is something wrong?" she tried to circumvent his obvious anger with the natural questions one asked of an unexpected visitor, but Rand was having none of it.

"You can answer my question first! What the hell are you doing here?"

"Ahh...I'd better get going." Vincent cleared his throat, taking one look at Rand and making an immediate decision. He was almost positive he'd have a better chance of survival if he stepped in the way of a flow of lava than face the eruption he sensed was barely contained within the hostile man who was looming over their table. "I'll see you later, Julie. I've got to get some sleep before going back to the site."

9

"WHO WAS THAT?" Rand demanded angrily, jamming both hands into the back pockets of his jeans as he watched Vince's hurried retreat from the room.

"That was Dr. Vincent Parmegelli from the Carlton Institute. If you hadn't been so rude, he might have stayed around long enough for me to introduce him," Julie retorted, her temper rapidly rising to meet Rand's. "What's the matter with you anyway? You're behaving like an idiot."

Rand didn't answer her question but took hold of her elbow and pulled her up out of her chair. Picking up her purse from the table and tucking it under his arm, he said, "We can discuss my supposed rudeness and my idiotic behavior once we're back at the villa. I've already stopped by your hotel and picked up your things."

"You've what?" Julie's incredulous expression made absolutely no impression on the man who was swiftly propelling her toward the door.

"You heard me. I assume that jump suit you're wearing and this purse are the only belongings you brought up here with you."

"I don't care what you—" she began, but broke off when she saw that they'd drawn the attention of several other occupants in the room.

"Rand! People are staring!" She lowered her voice so as not to be overheard, but her tone was fierce. "Where do you think you're taking me?"

"You can make this hard or make it easy," he muttered, clearly conveying his anger.

Julie tried to wrench free of his grasp. He tightened his grip on her elbow to counteract her resistance. "But you're coming with me."

"Leaving the observatory at a time like this would be madness. I'm not taking another step unless you tell me what this is all about." The rubber soles of Julie's shoes squeaked on the floor as she attempted to halt their steady progress toward the door.

Confused by Rand's strong-arm tactics, embarrassed that the other people in the room were avidly watching, she was also incensed that nothing she said appeared to be getting through to him. "You've got plenty of explaining to do, mister."

Rand looked down at his reluctant captive, saw the storm in her blue-green eyes and the stubborn set to her chin. He immediately took action, ensuring the only outcome he was willing to accept. "I warned you, lady," he gritted harshly, then bent down. When he straightened back up, Julie was safely stowed over his shoulder and the speed of their departure was greatly facilitated.

By the time Julie had regained her breath after Rand's unexpected action, they were through the cafeteria doors. The chuckles from the amused people observing Rand's totally juvenile maneuver echoed in her ears as she was carried down the hallway to the stairs. She would never be able to show her face here again. It was going to take years for her to live this incident down.

At first she was much too angry to struggle. Then, when a surge of adrenaline rushed through her body, she still didn't put up a fight. She knew without a doubt that in his present state of mind Rand would humiliate her even further if she did what she wanted to do and started kicking and screaming. If he could try something like this, he was obviously capable of anything. She felt like an outraged Victorian heroine being carried off by the high-handed hero in one of their mothers' historical novels.

When they were halfway up the stairs to the first floor, Vince Parmegelli hailed her from the bottom step. "Hey, Julie! I'll call L.A. and tell Dr. Lloyd that a personal crisis came up and you were...eh...forced to leave us for a while."

"Do something, Vince. Stop him," Julie sputtered desperately, lifting her head from the small of Rand's back but unable to see through the thick curtain of her hair.

"Not me, honey," Vince called back cheerfully, his voice breaking on a laugh. "Your man's got fifty pounds on me and my mama didn't raise no fool."

Incensed by her supposed friend's cowardly desertion, Julie muttered a most derogatory name under her breath. Rand heard her and observed snidely, "You said it, not I. Still, I'll give the man credit. He's got enough sense not to get in my way."

At that, Julie made one last try to enlist Vince's help. "Please, Vince. Call security," she wailed, but he remained where he was, a wide, infuriating grin on his face.

She arched her back and pulled her hair aside but all she got for the effort was an off-center glimpse of Kim White. At least she looked a bit more concerned and Julie's hope of rescue shone a trifle more brightly. The hope withered and died completely when Kim inquired, "You are the guy who's been stamped with the Stites Seal of Parental Approval, and not some crazy, aren't you?"

"In my case, those two descriptions are interchangeable," Rand tossed back over his free shoulder as he reached the top step. Not pausing for further questions, he strode through the lobby and proceeded toward the front entrance.

"Rand! Put me down right now!" Julie ordered as he stepped on the electronic sensors and the double doors slid open. "How could you embarrass me like this? Humiliate me in front of my colleagues?"

No answer.

"Damn you," she berated, finally giving in to the urge to hit him. Pounding on his back with her fists, she continued, "Because of you my friends are going to make me the butt of their jokes for months to come."

"I don't give a damn about those people," Rand snarled, not putting her down until they were a good ten yards from the building.

When she was steady on her feet, he renewed his grip on her arm, then pointed to the twin rivers of flaming lava flowing toward Hilo. "Those so-called friends of yours can laugh all the way to the grave, and that's exactly where they're going if they don't follow the civil defense warnings that have been on the radio for the past twenty-four hours. You, however, won't be with them when they're turned into a pile of burned cinders."

During her ignominious tenure as a sack of meal draped over Rand's shoulder, Julie had learned that the adult Rand was just as strong as he looked. No matter what things had been like when they'd been children, no matter how often she'd bested him, her strength was no longer a match for his. Since a physical attempt to stop him would prove utterly useless, she decided to appeal to his reason, that is if he still had any.

"You can't be serious," she began, foolishly allowing a withering note of sarcasm to taint her conciliatory tone. "Every person gathered here is a professional, a well-informed, dedicated scientist. Those of us in the field know far more about the dangers involved here than any radio announcer."

"Is that so?" Rand inquired evenly.

Julie was encouraged by his mild tone and failed to notice the revealing twist of his lips. "Yes it is," she reiterated firmly. "Honestly, Rand. You should know better than to believe all you hear. There was absolutely no need for these hysterics. I can't understand what got into you."

"Look over there." He gestured with his hand. "Do you see that helicopter revving up in the parking lot?"

Julie frowned at the abrupt change in subject but complied with his wishes. When she saw the craft in question, she shook her head, sure that Rand had made yet another wrong assumption. This concern for her welfare was sweet but misguided.

She was so exasperated with him, she had no idea how condescending she sounded when she said, "They've been in and out of here all day. Use your head, Rand. This place is surrounded by reporters and photographers. The commercial flights are shut down to keep the tourists away."

"And just why is that?" he inquired with a triumphant smirk.

"To cut down on the crowds so those who know what they're doing aren't impeded in their efforts," Julie returned, refusing to admit that safety was a factor in the precautionary measure. She knew the residents weren't fleeing the island in droves. A few people had left, but there were always those who expected the worst in any situation. Firmly she declared, "That copter isn't here because an evacuation is underway."

"But one is," Rand corrected curtly. "I hired that machine, and right now, if you've got any sense in that scientific brain of yours, you'll walk over there and get in." He didn't wait for her refusal but began striding toward the parking lot. Because he still held her arm, she was obliged to accompany him.

"Do you want my help to climb up or will you do it yourself?" he asked coldly when they were standing beneath the whirring blades of the helicopter.

Julie took one look at his face and decided that the colossal argument they were going to have could wait until they were back at the villa. Perhaps he'd have cooled off enough by then to be reasonable. Once she'd convinced him that she'd never been in any danger and given him a good piece of her mind, she'd return to the observatory and face the inevitable razzing of her colleagues. No matter how well-meaning his concern, Rand had to realize that she wouldn't tolerate this kind of interference in her work. Furthermore, even if there had been any real danger, she wouldn't have appreciated his cave-man-style rescue.

She could barely comprehend that he'd actually hired a helicopter, gone to her hotel, retrieved her belongings and then dragged her bodily out of the observatory as if she had no say in the matter at all. What kind of man would go to such mind-boggling lengths? A man in love, was the first response that sprang into her mind. Maybe Rand was as much in love with her as she was with him....

She dared to glance back at him as he assisted her through the door of the copter, but saw no sign of that heartwarming sentiment in his strong features. A dark fury raged in his eyes, his lips were fixed in a forbidding line and his jaw looked as if it had been cut from hard marble. Where was the lighthearted, devil-may-care companion who had been her loving guide through Eden? Where was the laughing clown who had danced the hula for her? Gripped by a sudden feeling of desolation, she quickly looked away.

It didn't take long for them to settle in the rear of the four-passenger craft. However, their takeoff was delayed because Julie couldn't seem to fasten her seat belt. Her fingers were shaking too badly. She'd never ridden in a helicopter before and was experiencing an attack of nerves. At least that's what she told Rand when he snatched the buckle away from her and fastened it himself.

"You don't have to be so rough," she complained as he yanked the strap until the wide material cut into her waist. "And you can stop looking like a thundercloud. I came with you. Isn't that what you wanted?"

"I'm not sure anymore," Rand replied in a voice that held the sting of a lash. "I know you don't think it's necessary, but I promised your folks you'd call when we get in. They got in touch with me as soon as they heard about the eruption. They're worried sick. Like myself, they aren't experts in the field. We were all dumb enough to worry about you."

"I never said you were dumb," Julie replied tightly, but then the chopper lifted away from the ground and zoomed off at such a sharp angle her stomach came up in her throat. She clapped both hands over her mouth and they stayed there until she saw the whisper of a grin on Rand's lips.

"You insensitive jerk," she berated, dropping her hands to her lap and willing her stomach to calm down. "You were hoping I'd get sick, weren't you?"

"Misery loves company," Rand retorted softly, then turned away to stare out the window. Julie was more than happy to follow suit.

The flight to Maui took less than an hour, but the atmosphere inside the craft was so tense it seemed far longer to Julie. For her that hour was an eternity. The noise from the powerful motor and the rotating blades gave her a headache. But worse, the taut-lipped passenger seated beside her set off an even greater pain—the pain of heartache. Rand had always been able to get under her skin, but now, because she loved him, he truly had the power to make her suffer.

After that last brief comment, Rand had made no attempt to speak to her. Indeed, he hadn't even looked at her, staring fixedly out the window. She didn't understand what she'd done that had made him so angry. Maybe she had come off sounding superior when she'd made those remarks about the personnel at the observatory, but Rand wasn't usually so quick to take offense.

She could think of hundreds of times over the years when she'd implied he was far worse than dumb. Considering all the things she'd called him back then, he'd have taken that mild a blandishment as a compliment. But this time she was completely innocent. Her supposed denigration of his mental capabilities was purely a misassumption on his part. She hadn't meant to convey that impression at all. Even if she had, she didn't see why he didn't write it off to her obvious frustration. Surely he could see that his peremptory treatment of her had made her furious, and he knew full well how illogical and belligerent she could be when angered.

After a few more moments of morose contemplation, it dawned on her that Rand might be familiar with her displays of anger but she was no longer familiar with his. Recalling the bitter argument they'd had after meeting the Sellinghams and her expectation that he'd been plotting revenge when he'd had nothing of the sort in mind, she realized that Rand had changed almost beyond recognition. She certainly didn't know the cold, silent stranger seated next to her and she was beginning to think she'd erroneously endowed him with traits he'd once had as a child, when in actuality that person no longer existed.

Taking that premise a step further, she wondered if those marvelous days they'd spent on Maui would in any way resemble how things would be once they stepped outside their island paradise. If they did get together again back on the mainland, would she find the endearing, witty and sensitive Rand Maxwell who occupied her dreams, or the dour stranger who occupied the copter?

Her patience with him had completely run out by the time the cab they'd taken from the airport dropped them off at the villa. Hurt by the distant expression in his eyes and the uncaring look on his face, she forced a confrontation the instant they stepped foot in the door.

"Look." She demanded his attention. Striving for control, she said evenly and calmly, "I realize that you've gone to a lot of expense and trouble to get me here, but if you continue behaving this way I'll turn right around and go back. You're not my father, Rand. Why don't you leave the parental censure to him?"

"All right." Rand shrugged and dropped her overnight bag on the floor. Turning his back on her, he walked across the living room and gazed out the sliding glass doors. "I owe you an apology, Julie. I'll make it as soon as you call your folks and tell them you're okay."

Julie was very much tempted to say that her phone call to Ohio could wait until after the two of them had cleared the air, but something in his voice prevented her from making the suggestion. His words held a note of finality, almost as if he was going to explain his behavior to her, ask her to understand, then tell her goodbye. If that was so, she didn't think she'd be capable of having a normal conversation with her parents. The desolate feeling she'd experienced in the helicopter doubled in intensity as she went into her bedroom and picked up the phone.

Rand had been right. Her parents had been extremely worried. It took some time to convince them that she'd never been in any danger. Once that was accomplished, they began to understand some of her enthusiasm over the eruption and wanted to know all the details. Considering the way Rand had sounded when he'd told her to make the call, Julie didn't want to linger long on the phone. She told her folks that she and Rand had reservations for dinner and had to leave if they were going to get to the restaurant on time. After promising to call the next morning, she hung up the receiver and went to join Rand in the living room.

He hadn't moved from his position by the doors where he was still staring through the glass. They had a lovely view of the ocean, but Julie was sure he wasn't watching the foamy white surf hit the beach. "Rand?" she murmured gently, trying not to startle him as she came to stand beside him. "What's wrong? I know whatever's bothering you goes far beyond that show we put on at the observatory."

"I overreacted today," Rand stated quietly. "I care about you, Julie. I listened to all those bulletins, viewed the awesome power of that eruption, the lava heading towards Hilo, and all I could think about was getting you out of there. I knew you'd argue about it and I refused to waste time listening. As I saw it, you were in danger. I'd never have been able to live with myself or look your parents in the eye again if I didn't do something about it."

"I understand that, Rand," Julie conceded. "But you've got to understand that, where my job is concerned, neither you, my parents, nor anyone else has the right to interfere. I wouldn't presume to tell you how to give a lecture."

Rand immediately bit out, "Dammit, Julie. That's hardly the same thing. My lecture hall is not about to explode or be covered with hot lava, and if it was I'd wish to God someone would get me out of there."

By sheer force of will, Julie refrained from losing her temper. Through her teeth, she grated, "That's your evaluation of my situation, but as I told you before nothing of the kind was about to happen."

"That's probably what the people of Pompeii said," he muttered in exasperation.

Julie ignored the reference. "Give me a little credit," she demanded. "If I'd thought there was any real danger, I would have called for a helicopter myself. Now, because of you, I'm missing out on a major event."

"You little fool. You're going back, aren't you." Rand's remark was more a statement than a question.

"Of course I am," she retorted angrily, her fury finally outweighing her better judgment. "And if you were me, you'd do the same thing."

"That's where you're wrong," he declared sarcastically. "I try to think about other people's feelings instead of my own."

"What's that supposed to mean?" she flung back.

"Anybody who knows you is scared to death that you'll play this thing true to form. If your revered associates at Carlton told you you were the best person for the job, you'd go right up to the top of that damned volcano and jump in."

Without giving her the chance to defend herself against his vitriolic attack, he blazed, "If you'd heard yourself talking to that Italian hotshot, you'd know why I hauled you out of there. He, at least, had the good sense to point out that it was hell that close. You couldn't talk about anything except how great it would be to get a firsthand look. You can't wait to get your chance to go up there."

"I wouldn't be allowed," she informed him tersely.

"And just when have you bowed to anybody's rules and regulations but your own?" he snarled back at her. "You were already figuring out a way to get up there. It was written all over your face."

"I'm getting a little sick of your thinking you can read my mind, Skeeter Maxwell. Besides, what I choose to do, stupid or not, is my decision. I'm not going to say this again," she warned, her voice matching the level of her rage. "Nobody comes between me and my work. I've spent years getting to this point in my career, and I won't let anyone stand in my way."

"In other words, nothing but your career really matters to you," he charged, his eyes coldly condemning.

Stung by his scathing assessment of her, Julie's temper wavered. "That's not true," she denied brokenly. "You matter to me, Rand, and so does my family."

"Then if I asked you to stay here with me, you wouldn't go back to Hilo?"

More than her safety was at issue here, and Julie weighed her response carefully. "I would hope you wouldn't ask that of me," she stated, watching his face for some indication of his thoughts.

The Rand she thought she knew was open, but this man's features were unreadable. In an attempt to force him to reveal his motives, she placed the ball firmly back in his court. "Are you sure you want to force me to make that kind of choice?"

"I have only two days left here," he informed her bitterly. Then, softening noticeably, he offered, "I was hoping to spend them with you."

"I'd love that, too," Julie's eyes begged him to understand. "We have tonight, Rand. I'm with you now. Let's not waste this precious time fighting."

Rand longingly studied her face, looking deep into her eyes. Finally he uttered a resigned sigh and accepted her overture. With the grace and power of an island chieftan, he swung her off her feet and into his arms. "Tonight, my goddess of fire, you belong completely to me."

He carried her down the hall to her bedroom and settled her on the bed. Falling heavily beside her, his hands immediately sought the buttons of her jump suit, and as he slowly undid them, his eyes never left hers. By the time he had finished the deliberately provocative exercise, Julie was trembling beneath his touch.

"That's right. Burn for me, Julie," he murmured in a dark, velvety voice as his fingers trailed along the softness of her exposed breasts.

"Rand." She breathed his name joyously as he bent to kiss a pink-tipped mound. "I do. You know I do."

"Yes," he growled passionately, his warm tongue flicking across her nipple until it hardened with desire. He slid the material of her jump suit away from her shoulders, taking his time as he pulled it past her hips and down over her thighs. Her legs moved with restless abandon until he shifted his weight to anchor her more firmly beneath him. Lying half on top of her, he removed the last scrap of her clothing.

Letting her feel the strength in him, he rasped thickly, "Tonight I want everything you have to give. And it works both ways. Whatever you take is yours."

"Then I'll take everything," she warned him recklessly.

He rolled away from her in order to remove his clothes. Julie watched the impatient urgency in his movements, saw the deep hunger in his eyes that mirrored what she felt in her soul. He, like no other man on earth, made her give thanks that she was a woman.

Shivering with need, she urged him down beside her, fingers tugging on his hair and her body arching into his. She conveyed all the passion she was feeling in her kiss and gloried in the sensation of his heart beating heavily between her breasts.

He was fully aroused, ready for her, and she had never been more ready for him. The heat of his body, the heady scent of him and the intoxicating taste that was uniquely his made her dizzy with wanting. His searching caresses were rapidly bringing her to the brink of fulfillment, but before the sheer ecstasy could build to the point of no return, he stopped. Julie opened her eyes and stared up at him.

"I want to hear you admit something, Julie," he said, his voice revealing his strain. "I need the words more than anything."

"What words?" she uttered in a halting whisper.

"I need you to say that, at this moment, I mean everything to you. I need to know that when I take you, you belong to me."

"You know I do," she breathed, and then his mouth came down hard on hers.

He took control of her body, her mind and her heart with sure strokes. She clung to him, meeting and retreating until the pleasure became so intense that neither could resist. Together they flew directly into the maelstrom of sweet torment that was fulfillment.

Throughout the night she did indeed take everything she wanted, and so did Rand. He pulled every response from her that she had to offer, then adored her for each one. He made her his over and over again until her eyes closed on a last exhausted whisper of his name.

A gentle night breeze heavy with the fragrance of flowers was fanned by the palms that surrounded the villa. It floated over their bed and cloaked their moist skin in a soft blanket of perfume. Never more content, never more cherished, Julie nestled her head in the slope of Rand's shoulder and went to sleep.

Less than an hour later, a pink dawn painted the sky. Slowly, reluctantly, Rand eased his arm from beneath Julie's head. Once out of bed, he stood staring at her for a long time.

He knew he had to accept that his time in paradise was over. True to her word, she'd given him a night he'd never forget, but not once had she offered anything more. Her career came first, and he would only destroy what was between them if he tried to make her change her mind. At least if he left now he'd have a beautiful memory to take with him, one that wasn't tarnished by bitter recriminations and arguments.

He purposely made little noise as he got dressed and began packing. His suitcases were full and waiting at the door when Julie awakened and realized she was alone in the bed. "Where are you going, Rand?" She sat up quickly, her vision still clouded by sleep.

She brushed a hand across her eyes and propped herself against the headboard, drawing the sheet over her breasts. Instinctively she braced herself to withstand the heart-wrenching blast of reality she somehow knew had come to invade her idyll. With a strong sense of foreboding, she tried to focus on the nightmarish scene unfolding before her.

Reluctantly Rand came to stand at the foot of the bed. His expression was strained, his jaw tight as he said, "Goodbye, Julie. I won't make this hard on both of us by begging for something I can't have. What we've shared was good while it lasted. But I guess we both knew how it had to end."

Too stupefied to speak, Julie watched him turn on his heel, pick up his cases and walk out the door. She heard the tread of his feet as he moved through the living room, the whoosh of the door opening and the sharper click of its closing. The sound was cold and brutally final.

10

JULIE STARED out her office window at the row of palm trees that bordered Carlton Institute's front lawn. If she gazed at them long enough, she could almost imagine that she was back in Hawaii. The same ocean crashed against a shoreline not far from her window. The same breezes wafted the fronds of the towering palms. But she wasn't in Hawaii. She was in Los Angeles.

There were no exotic scents in the air. There was no secluded beach or romantic villa. There was no smiling, golden-eyed man to share the days and nights with. There was no Rand.

It had been months since that morning he'd left her alone, but the hurt hadn't lessened. "It was good while it lasted." His words came back to her over and over again, reminding her that what she'd believed would go on forever, he had brought to a brutal end. With no explanations, not even a backward glance, he had walked out of the door and out of her life.

For the first hour after his desertion, she'd been too stunned to move, to react, to feel. Then the tears had come, falling like a never-ending sheet of rain. Hours later, when she'd caught sight of herself in a mirror, her despair had turned to anger. No man, not even Rand, was worth the kind of suffering she'd seen reflected in the glass.

She'd bathed her swollen eyes, given herself a stern lecture and by that evening was back on the Big Island. She threw herself into her work with a vengeance. She should have known that Skeeter the Cheater would play her false. Even so, she'd foolishly given him her heart.

She'd sensed from the beginning that she was a challenge he'd wanted to conquer and all too easily she'd handed him a total victory. He'd allowed no quarter and she'd surrendered unconditionally. She'd have to live with that painful knowledge for the rest of her life.

That insight had been the source of the fury that had compelled her to work long hours, never allowing her thoughts to stray from the job at hand. However, once she'd returned to the mainland, completed her dissertation and oral examinations, she'd not been able to cast her love for Rand aside. Her anger had melted away and been replaced by soft memories. It was the beauty of those remembrances that led to the desolation she was still experiencing. No matter how many friends she had, no one could fill the space Rand occupied inside her heart.

Julie closed her eyes for a moment, then reached for the empty coffee mug at the corner of her desk. If she didn't start work soon, she'd never be able to get away for Thanksgiving. She felt a great need to go home this year. Perhaps by returning to Granville she could dispel the feeling of loneliness that had plagued her for months. She got up from her desk and started down the hall to the vending machines.

"If you're on the way to the coffee machine, would you mind bringing a cup back for me?" Vince called as Julie passed the open door of his office.

"Not at all," Julie acquiesced as she always did, even knowing that as surely as the sun would rise again in the east, Vince wouldn't have any change to repay her.

Minutes later she placed a Styrofoam cup of steaming caramel-colored liquid on his desk. "Cream, no sugar. Right?"

"Right." Vince smiled up at her. He leaned to one side, fished in his pants pocket, brought out a handful of coins and handed them to her.

"This can't be for the coffee," Julie teased, dramatizing her shock by widening her eyes in an exaggerated fashion.

"Part of my new image," he revealed, unruffled by her display.

"Part?" Julie queried, raising one brow. "Except for costing me a fortune in coffee, I rather liked the old Vince. What was the matter with him?"

"He was a selfish, egotistical SOB and you well know it," Vince said in self-contempt.

"Uh-oh. I have the distinct feeling you didn't come to this conclusion on your own."

"Certainly not," he confirmed. "We self-centered types think we're perfect."

Julie set aside any ideas of rushing back to her windowless cubicle at the end of the hall. The topographical studies of the Pacific chain waiting on her desk could wait a little longer. Vince wasn't the only one working on a new image.

Her job was still just as important to her as it had always been, but she'd been working on the other facets of her life. Since Hawaii, she'd rearranged her priorities, recognizing the truth in the philosophy that no man is an island. Humans were a social species in need of close association with other humans. Once accepting that truth, she had opened up and developed real friendships with many of her associates at the Institute—especially Vince.

Vince was the only one at Carlton Institute who had witnessed Rand's "rescue," and he had still been on the Big Island when she'd returned two days later. He'd run interference for her whenever anyone attempted to tease her about it, and after the first day no one dared bring it up. She hadn't been able to talk about what had transpired between her and Rand until weeks later when they were back on the mainland. It had been Vince she'd turned to, instinctively knowing he'd be the best listener she could have found.

"Care to talk about it?" she invited. After closing the door, she seated herself in the only other chair in his office.

She owed him. Being there for a friend was a part of her campaign toward a new image. Vince wasn't the only one who'd been accused of being self-centered.

"Nothing to tell, really." He toyed with the pens and pencils stuck in a mug on his desk. The nervous action was out of character and Julie sensed he was hedging. She waited patiently, just as he had done with her months ago.

Finally after several moments he began, "I'm sure you know that Kim White and I spent a lot of time together in the islands."

Julie nodded and settled more comfortably into her chair. In true scientific fashion, Vince went right to the core of his problem. With complete honesty, he admitted that his reputation with women was for the most part true. While he'd gone into an affair with Kim with his usual cavalier attitude, somehow it hadn't been as easy to forget her as he'd expected. Something about the tall, vivacious Hawaiian had really gotten to him.

Unfortunately, the young woman in question wanted nothing more to do with him. Evidently Kim was turning the tables on the Carlton Institute's resident Casanova. She was treating their affair very casually, and Vince's feelings were far from casual. Kim had bluntly told him that it had been fun while it lasted but she had no intention of getting serious about him. She'd informed him in no uncertain terms that he was too fond of himself to ever find room for anyone else in his life.

"You've heard the old saw that you pay for everything in this life," Vince stated when he'd finished. "I'm paying now."

"When did you last see her?" Julie asked, feeling guilty that she'd been the very one who had warned Kim of Vince's reputation.

"I flew over there about a month ago. When I tried to renew our relationship she let me have it."

"Was that the first time you contacted her since we left Hawaii?"

Sheepishly, Vince admitted that it was.

"Well, no wonder she was so mad at you," Julie told him, her guilt evaporating. Kim's handling of Vince was exactly what the man needed. It was just possible that Julie's revelations to Kim had indirectly been to his benefit. "What did you expect? That she'd been waiting with bated breath just in case you showed up?"

"I told you I was an SOB."

Julie resisted agreeing with him. He looked too defeated for her to heap more abuse on his head. "Are you willing to humble yourself a little bit?" she asked gently.

"I don't know, Julie. When I went over there, she didn't have the time or the inclination to spend more than a few minutes with me. Do you think I should try again?"

"I can't advise you, Vince," Julie replied honestly, thinking about the mess she'd made with Rand. "You'll have to decide whether what you feel for Kim is worth fighting for. If it is, then I'd say you'd better try again."

"That's what you'd do, huh?"

"If I cared enough," Julie responded thoughtfully.

Vince grinned, giving her a full blast of his twinkling white teeth and deep dark eyes. "So why haven't you?"

"I beg your pardon?"

"You know who I'm talking about," he drawled. "The guy who thought so much of you he dragged you away from the jaws of death. The one you cried over," he added as if she needed another reminder.

"What he did was stupid," Julie judged, her mouth tightening to keep her lips from quivering.

"Some might say it was very romantic. Sort of like the white knight charging in to rescue the fair damsel from the fire-breathing dragon," Vince analogized, receiving a sharp glare from Julie.

"He wasn't all wrong, you know," he continued more seriously. "None of us knew exactly what was going to happen. Considering that two volcanoes were going off at once, there was the chance that the whole island would go."

"You didn't believe that then and you don't now," she scoffed. "You're just sticking up for him because you belong to the same fraternity—Macho Alpha Lowdown Exasperepsilon!"

Vince laughed. "Very clever," he complimented but wouldn't be sidetracked. "I'll grant you that he may have overreacted, but he acted out of love."

Julie slowly shook her head in denial, but Vince was not to be swayed. "The male of any species doesn't always act rationally when he's in love. When the initial excitement wears off, he may regret his actions. Then, if he's been made to feel particularly foolish, he'll crawl back into his cave to lick his wounds."

"Are you describing Rand or yourself?" Julie gibed impatiently.

"Maybe both," he replied. "We members of M.A.L.E. are very sensitive, actually, and need some encouragement to emerge from our caves. Take my word for it. I've been living with the bats so long they're starting to look good to me."

"Kim will help you out of there if you show her your reformed self," Julie declared, laughing.

"So will that man of yours," Vince tendered. "If you'll admit your feelings and go after him."

"There aren't any feelings to admit," Julie lied.

"Julie, Julie, Julie," Vince scolded, shaking his head. "You haven't mentioned his name again until today, but those blue eyes of yours have been giving away more than you think. You care, my dear Dr. Stites. You care very much."

Julie shifted uncomfortably, worried her lower lip with her teeth. Vince was right and there was no use trying to deny it again. However, she'd been the one in the cave licking her wounds. Rand had walked out on her, not the other way around. She wasn't going to embarrass herself by going after him. That would be an exercise in futility.

"I thought you asked for my advice," she accused. "I seem to be receiving more than I'm giving."

"Have you called him?" Vince persisted doggedly, totally ignoring her accusation.

"No, but he hasn't called me, either," Julie answered defensively.

Vince tilted his chair backward, rested his elbows on the arms and tented his fingers. He studied her for a long moment, then pronounced, "You're both fools."

"Isn't that the pot calling the kettle black?" Julie fired back.

"Touché," Vince acknowledged. "Are you going home for Thanksgiving?"

Julie nodded.

"Will he be there?"

"No," Julie supplied too quickly, and was rewarded with a very knowing grin from Vince. Unable to withstand the cross-examination any longer, Julie went on the offensive. "You could always spend Thanksgiving in Hawaii. Swallow your pride, you turkey, and try again with Kim."

"I could eat a little crow, I suppose." Vince smirked and dropped his hands to his desk. "Thanks Julie."

"You're welcome." Smiling, she suggested, "Send her roses and call her before you show up."

"You think that'll do it?" he asked, a glimmer of hope evidenced by his crooked smile.

"Not many women can resist roses. Maybe a little bit of poetry," she added wistfully as she prepared to leave. "Good luck." She reached for the doorknob.

"And to you," he returned. "Take your own advice, doctor."

"Roses and poetry?"

"Whatever works."

"YOU MUST HAVE BEEN UP before dawn, mom." Julie stumbled sleepily down the two steps that led into the kitchen. A shower hadn't quite erased the cobwebs from her brain, and her body was definitely still operating on California time. She poured herself a cup of coffee and leaned one hip against the butcher-block counter.

She closed her eyes and savored the delicious aromas that filled the huge keeping room at the back of the big old house. "I could smell that turkey all the way upstairs. Why didn't you roust me out before now? I planned on helping."

Angela Stites lifted a pumpkin pie from one of the twin ovens built into the brick wall beside the kitchen's enormous fireplace. "I didn't have the heart, dear. You had such a long flight and arrived so late, I knew you could use the sleep."

A pecan pie took up the space in the oven just vacated by the pumpkin. After closing the door and adjusting the temperature, Angela turned her full attention to her daughter. "Sit down, Julie. Your father left you a few muffins and I think they're still warm," she said with an enticing smile. "Can I get you anything else?"

Julie needed no urging to settle herself on the cushioned window seat of the breakfast bay. Immediately she started slathering butter and marmalade on one of her mother's delicious bran muffins. "Mmm, nobody makes these like you do. I try but they just don't turn out the same."

Angela tossed another log on the grate. "It's hardly a secret recipe, Julie," she remarked absently as she poked at the coals. "I don't know why you have so much trouble making them turn out right." Frowning, she watched a single flame taste the fresh log, then she nodded in satisfaction as it caught and flared.

"I just don't have your magic touch." Julie reached for another muffin. "Or maybe it's this kitchen. They just taste better in here."

Angela poured herself a mug of coffee and joined her daughter at the scrubbed-pine table. "Probably the wood smoke that usually flavors them," she muttered, casting another glance at the fire to assure herself it hadn't gone out. "The fires I set always smoke too much. I should've had Will set it before he left."

"Where is dad?" Julie tucked one leg beneath her and glanced out the window at the bird feeders.

She smiled when a flashy male cardinal drove away the timid little juncos that had been gorging themselves on the seed. Looking at the trees and bushes in the backyard, Julie spied the cardinal's mate waiting in the thicket of the forsythia hedge that lined the yard. She'd missed Ohio—the abundant cardinals, the hint of frost in the air and the dusting of snow on bare branches. It was good to be home.

"Your father's at his office, I suspect," Angela informed her with a long-suffering sigh. "No matter what I say to him, he won't slow down. He hasn't had any trouble since that incident last spring, so he's gone back to thinking he's Superman."

"You really should go to Hawaii. I guarantee some time at the Maui villa will relax you," Julie suggested, trying to forget that her last days there had done just the opposite.

"We are. I've already got plane reservations for the first day of the Christmas break. If you want to spend Christmas with us this year, you'll have to fly west rather than east. I'll even send you the fare for a Christmas present."

Julie smiled, genuinely happy her parents were going to take advantage of the Angel Sylver purchase. "No, I think you and dad should enjoy it alone. It's—" She stopped before saying that the villa was very romantic and that her parents could have a second honeymoon there. That might very well have raised questions she didn't want to answer. "It's Thanksgiving. Even dad doesn't go to his office on a holiday," she covered.

"Not usually, but someone called and out he went, saying he had to pick up something. You know your father." Angela shook her head. "I just hope he doesn't get so distracted that he loses track of time. The switchboard's closed at the university for the weekend, and I won't be able to call him and remind him to come home for dinner. I'm planning on serving around two o'clock."

Julie glanced at the old Seth Thomas mantel clock. "That gives him another three hours. Tecumseh won't keep him that long," she added with a twinkling grin.

Her mother laughed. It was a joke they'd long shared at the professor's expense. Once he'd taken Angela to a theater, and just as they arrived, he'd realized he'd left their tickets in his desk drawer. Leaving her in the comfort of the lobby, he'd dashed through the rain and driven back to his office.

A lengthy piece of research revealing new details about the famous Shawnee Indian chief's life had been lying atop his desk and it caught his eye. He'd become so engrossed in the article that he'd forgotten all about Angela, and she'd had to take a taxi home. Since then Tecumseh had facetiously been blamed every time Will was excessively late.

Eyeing the row of covered dishes on the counter waiting their turn in the oven, Julie commented, "Looks like your usual feast—enough for an army. Who all's coming today?"

"Just Sylvia," Angela supplied with a small shrug. "But I have to be prepared in case one or more of your father's students couldn't go home for the holidays. It always amazes me how he knows when one of those kids is stuck alone in the dorm."

She rose and picked up the napkin-lined basket from the table. Giving it a shake, she said, "There's one left. Here, finish it off for me." She plucked the muffin from its linen nest and placed it on Julie's plate.

"Mom," Julie groaned, already buttering the muffin, "I won't have room for dinner."

"Nonsense," Angela quickly negated, pushing the marmalade jar within easier reach as she left the eating area. "You've always had a healthy appetite and never gain an excess pound."

"I probably will today," Julie moaned, casting another look at the array of food on the counter. "I definitely will today."

Busily cleaning a head of lettuce at the sink, Angela called over the sound of running water. "You could always work your dinner off with a long walk or have a fast game of one-on-one like you used to. The hoop's still up and you can probably find a basketball in the garage."

"Mother..." Julie warned, her suspicious glare going unnoticed by Angela whose back was turned. Julie and Rand had spent many past Thanksgivings playing basketball while their mothers chatted and their fathers fell asleep in front of the television after the sumptuous feast. "Just who do you have in mind for me to play with?"

"No one in particular, dear," Angela replied, her attention still on the lettuce. She shut off the tap and turned away from the sink. It was then that she saw Julie's face. "Oh no, Julie. I haven't set you up again. I learned my lesson last time. I was just thinking of the student your father is probably bringing home with him."

She wiped her hands on her apron, picked up the coffee pot and brought it to the table. She filled the two mugs and sat down. "You've never said what really happened in Hawaii, darling, and I'm not going to pry. Believe me, Sylvia and I are so sorry for what we did to you two. Your father warned us, but we wouldn't listen. We let our own dreams and wishful thinking take us right down the road to disaster."

"It wasn't exactly a disaster, mom," Julie soothed. "I know you meant well but. . ." She trailed off, turning her attention back to the view beyond the bowed windows, afraid her mother might see the heartache she always felt when she was reminded of that time.

Experiencing Rand's lovemaking was hardly a disaster, except that it had spoiled her for any other man. She'd never be sorry for that time spent with him, only that it had ended. He'd taught her to play, to open herself fully to other people. However, she was paying a heavy tuition for those lessons now.

"Butt is exactly what we did." Angela's voice held a note of self-derision. "Sylvia and I butted into your lives, and we had no right. I know something happened that's very painful for both of you. Rand gets the same look on his face that you have right now, and he's just as closemouthed."

"You've talked to him? He's been here?" Julie was unable to keep the eagerness out of her voice. Any knowledge of Rand, even secondhand, might fill part of the void in her heart.

"Of course," Angela replied matter-of-factly. "He spent about a week with Sylvia on his way back to New York, and then he was here again at the end of the summer before the fall semester began. Rand and your father are great friends, you know. I'd like to think he regards me as a friend, also. Sylvia feels the same way about you."

Angela's gaze dropped as she picked at a snag in the terry-cloth apron spread across her lap. "At least Syl hopes she's still your friend. She cares so much for you, Julie. She's always thought of you as the daughter she never had."

"Just like you think of Rand," Julie observed softly.

"Yes. Well..." Angela sighed wearily. "Syl and I will just have to resign ourselves to the fact that our children can't be expected to go along with our fantasies. We married you off in the cradle but have since realized arranged marriages belong to another century. From now on we're just going to write about them."

With slightly forced cheer, she went on, "So let's not waste any more time hashing over what might have been. There's still lots to do, and now that you're up, awake, nourished and willing, I'm putting you to work."

Two hours later Julie had finished setting the table with freshly polished silver flatware when the doorbell rang. It was Sylvia Maxwell. The woman's eyes, brown inlaid with gold, were so like Rand's that Julie had to blink away the image of his face that had superimposed itself over his mother's.

Sylvia offered a hesitant greeting when she saw who had answered the door. Julie experienced a moment's hesitation, herself. The emotion fled as soon as she realized Sylvia was alone. Controlling her leaping stomach, she flung the door wide and with a mixture of relief and disappointment welcomed Rand's mother.

Julie caught the slender woman up in a warm hug. "Hello, Sylvia. Gee, it's good to see you."

Sylvia returned the hug and kissed Julie's cheek. She bent to pick up a wicker basket before entering the house. "Dr. Stites, you're even more lovely than the last time I saw you."

"Thank you, and I'd like to return the compliment," Julie responded merrily. She took Sylvia's coat and ushered her to the back of the house.

"You didn't need to bring anything, Syl," Angela reproved mildly when she saw the basket her friend was carrying.

"I know, but I just couldn't resist. Once the manuscript was printed, copied and sent off, I still had a little time on my hands so I got busy in my kitchen." She extracted a three-tiered cake. "Blackberry-jam cake," she announced. "I haven't had the time to make it for ages, and I thought Thanksgiving was a good excuse to indulge myself."

"You're not the only one you're indulging," Julie commented, licking her lips. Her anticipatory gleam grew when she saw Sylvia produce a lemon meringue pie and a loaf of Dilly bread.

"Where's Will?" Sylvia asked as she donned an apron and prepared to pitch in with the preparations.

"Right here." Willard Stites stepped through the back doorway of the kitchen. "Smells awfully good in here," he observed, crossing to the fire and holding his chilled hands out to the warmth.

He turned his back to the flames and said, "You'd better set another place. I've brought someone home with me."

Angela and Julie exchanged knowing winks and looked to the doorway. The smile of welcome instantly dropped from Julie's face. The tall, dark-haired man who paused in the entry was neither a student nor a stranger.

"Don't just stand there, Rand," Will instructed. "Get over here and warm up."

Sylvia was across the polished wood floor in seconds to be caught up in her son's arms. "Rand! Rand, you said you wouldn't be coming," she exclaimed joyously.

"I was able to clear up some work and was lucky enough to catch a flight out this morning," Rand explained, releasing his mother. He smiled warmly at Angela and nodded politely to Julie as if she was no more than a passing acquaintance.

"I'd intended to surprise you by driving myself from the airport, but all the rental cars were taken," he continued while Sylvia pulled him farther into the room.

"I figured you'd probably be busy baking or something even though Angela's laying out the spread this year. I called Will and asked him to come pick me up." He directed an apologetic nod toward Angela. "Sorry to take him away from you this morning."

"No apologies necessary," Angela dismissed. "We're just glad you could make it."

Rand acted on Will's invitation to warm himself by the fire, passing within inches of Julie. "Hi," he said lightly. "It's good to see you."

"Hi," Julie returned, hoping her voice sounded as even as his. Unable to look at him without wanting to throw herself into his arms, she picked up a tray of relishes. "I'll take this into the dining room, mom."

Hands closed behind his back, Rand stared into the fire, hoping everyone thought he was trying to warm up. Actually he was trying to control his strong physical reaction to seeing Julie again. When he'd boarded the plane at La Guardia, he hadn't expected to find her in Granville. She never went home for Thanksgiving. Will hadn't mentioned her until they'd been well away from Port Columbus. By that time it would have been ridiculous for him to beg off. Even though he'd been forewarned, the sight of her was still a shock.

He supposed he could make the best of it. After all, it was inevitable that he'd run into her sooner or later, considering the association his mother had with Julie's parents. He would have preferred, however, that the meeting had taken place some time in the distant future. It was too soon, far too soon, to look at her without remembering the softness of her lips, how her eyes spoke to him. He could still remember the feel of her hand tucked within his own, how her lush body had welcomed him....

He took a long sip of the brandy Will thrust into his hand and managed to exchange some small talk, but all the time his thoughts were on Julie. Damn! Why did she have to look so good?

Dressed in pale mauve slacks and a matching fuzzy sweater, she was delectable. Her skin was just as golden as it had been on the islands. She obviously hadn't been suffering one whit! But then, what did he expect?

She had her all-important career to fulfill her. With the newly earned Ph.D. behind her name, she was no doubt perfectly content with her life. It was proceeding exactly according to plan, a plan that had never included him. He'd been nothing but a short detour, and she had soon left him behind.

In the dining room, Julie sank down onto the nearest chair. How was she ever going to get through this day without making a total fool of herself? Rand certainly didn't look as if he'd just emerged from a dark cave where he'd been licking his wounds. He looked wonderful!

The mahogany V-neck sweater that stretched smoothly across his broad shoulders clearly outlined what she knew lay beneath. The brown-and-white pin-striped oxford shirt he wore beneath was open at the neck, revealing the strong cords she had kissed with such hunger. His camel flannel slacks skimmed his lean hips, hugged his muscular thighs and reminded her all too clearly of the strength he possessed.

The softly textured fabrics next to his large form would be warmed by his body, and the thought made her tremble. Her fingers tingled with remembered sensations. She had trailed them across those perfect shoulders, up his neck, and buried them in his luxuriant chestnut hair.

The sound of his slightly rough baritone carried from the kitchen, curled around her, caressed her as he spoke with her father, her mother, Sylvia—everyone but her. But then that was probably for the best. While he was having no trouble making intelligent conversation, she was a mass of quivering nerves and didn't trust her vocal cords.

Abruptly she got up from the table, rattling the crystal and silver. While arranging another place setting, she gave herself a stern lecture on poise. *If he could act so cool, calm and collected, then so could she*. Taking several deep steadying breaths, Julie returned to the kitchen.

Fortunately for her, pleasant before-dinner conversation was no longer necessary as the meal was about to be served and everyone was pressed into service bringing the food to the table. Thinking it would be better to sit on the same side as Rand so that she wouldn't have to look at him every time she raised her eyes from her plate, Julie took the chair beside his. In order to accommodate the bountiful feast, several leaves had been put in the table, so she and Rand were separated by at least two feet.

The trouble began when her father bowed his head for the blessing and reached for Julie's hand. It had always been the custom at the Stites's home that grace was recited in unison, all hands joined around the table. Julie had no choice but to extend hers to Rand just as she'd been forced to do years ago when their families had shared holiday dinners. This time she wasn't holding the cold, clammy paw of a skinny adolescent nerd, but the strong, capable hand of a man.

The familiar words of the prayer came easily to her lips, but her mind was elsewhere. Holding hands with Rand still felt like a fate worse than death, though this time it wasn't because he was trying to prove his bone-crushing strength under cover of the table. Her hand was enveloped in his, warmly, tenderly, completely.

When the prayer ended Rand didn't release her. Instead, he shifted his chair closer, then moved their clasped hands to his thigh. Julie thought she might faint as his warmth branded her palm.

When her father raised his wineglass to propose a toast, Julie was forced to pick up hers with her left hand, a hand that was trembling so badly she feared spilling the ruby liquid on her mother's best damask tablecloth. If that happened, every person at the table would be aware of how she was reacting to being this close to Rand.

"To the past and the many times we've shared," Will began, his gaze sweeping around the table. "May the future hold many more such gatherings."

"Hear, hear," everyone voiced the traditional response.

Only then, after a slight squeeze, did Rand release Julie's hand. Unable to help herself, she glanced at him. He'd once told her he could read her thoughts in her expression, and she tried to pull her gaze away before he read the love she still carried for him.

But for a brief moment, their eyes met and held. In that short span of time she imagined she saw a reflection of her own pain. But that couldn't be, she warned herself. That was just wishful thinking on her part, a selfish hope that he'd been as miserable for the past seven months as she had been.

"That was a lovely toast, Will," Sylvia remarked. She smiled across the table at her son. "And a lovely surprise. Thank you for making it possible for Rand to be with us today."

"Couldn't let him sit at the airport all day," Will said as he began carving the golden-brown turkey. "Besides, it's a blessing for me that he's here." He winked at Rand. "I'm counting on you to eat heartily, big fella. If you don't, I'll be eating leftover turkey until Christmas."

"I'll do my best," Rand vowed.

Evidence of his quick humor emerged in a flashing grin. He glanced once at Julie's hand then down at his thigh. "How about you, Julie? Can you manage a whole leg or will you be content to settle for a slice?"

"If you can, I can," Julie returned, praying that nobody else had picked up on the sexual connotation behind his question. She didn't understand why he was doing this. Did he still feel something for her, or was this some cruel form of retribution?

"I knew you wouldn't settle for a mere slice," he drawled, his amber-and-brown eyes glittering wickedly. "As I recall, you have a very healthy appetite." Then he brought up a subject everyone else had purposely avoided. "While we were in Hawaii, she was always hungry. It took some doing to keep up with her."

As Julie tried to hide her utter mortification, Sylvia added to her discomfiture. "Somehow I doubt that, Rand. You've never been known to skip a meal."

Rand's laugh was not so much for his mother's quip but for the interpretation he put upon it. "I'll have to admit," he supplied, "I indulged myself as much as she did."

Julie was relieved that the passing of plates heaped with turkey diverted the discussion from her "appetite." Serving dishes brimming with tempting, traditional delicacies quickly followed, and each time Rand placed a generous portion of something on his plate, he passed the dish to Julie with a challenging grin. She forced herself to respond each time with an equal or better serving accompanied by a "so there" expression. All the while she knew that Alka Seltzer would be her choice of after-dinner beverage. That is, if she didn't explode beforehand—just punishment for this kind of gluttony.

It was stupid to try to match Rand's consumption, and she knew she was going to pay dearly for entering into such a childish endurance match. Common sense told her that being far bigger than she, he had a greater capacity. She didn't know what would be proved by his inevitable triumph, but she was willing to concede it to him by the meal's end. Rand's plate was clear whereas hers still held several small mounds of assorted foods. Full to bursting, she pushed a forkful of scalloped corn around and around on her plate, having absolutely no success convincing her hand to bring it to her mouth.

"Don't do it," Rand counseled sagely when he saw her fork hesitate in midair. "You should always listen to what your body is trying to tell you. It always knows best. Pride and stubbornness will only get you misery."

Julie paled but managed, "You sound as if you speak from experience, Rand. Do you suffer from the sin of pride?"

BENEATH THE DANGLING STRINGS of the bent and rusted basketball hoop, Rand dribbled the ball in place. His eyes were bright with challenge as he stole a quick glance at his opponent. Without breaking the bouncing rhythm he'd set as soon as they'd stepped out onto the paved driveway, he taunted, "Are you ready?"

"Haven't we played enough games today?" Julie stood with her hands on her hips, frustration and exasperation stiffening her long limbs. "You've already won the glutton of the year award and proved you're the master of innuendo. What more do you want from me?"

"How about a more physical contest," Rand returned equably. "You used to love to wipe up the court with me. Think you can still do it?"

"I don't think it matters," Julie asserted, shoving her hands in the pockets of her jacket. She stared down at the old pair of sneakers she'd reluctantly put on when Rand had all but forced her to accompany him outside. "We're not kids anymore and another contest won't prove a thing. Don't you think we're getting a bit long in the tooth for this?"

Rand fired the ball across the driveway at her. Her hands flew out of her pockets and caught the ball before it slammed against her chest. He grinned, his eyes sparkling. Her naturally fast reflexes had come into play just as he'd expected.

Out of lifelong habit, she bounced the ball on the pavement, testing it's buoyancy. "It's like riding a bike. Once you learn, you never forget," she mused.

"We'll see. You've still got good hands, but how about your footwork?" Rand queried. "And stamina? Think you can still cut it?"

Even knowing that he was deliberately goading her, Julie had never been able to walk away from a head-on challenge. With a quick flex of her wrist, she sent the ball sailing in a perfect arc towards the hoop. It passed through the metal rim without even touching the edges.

"Ah, the infamous Stilts and her famous swish shot from the foul line. Bet you can't do it again." He retrieved the ball and tossed it back to her.

Without a word, Julie made the second basket as easily as she'd made the first, then issued a challenge of her own. "Want to bet money on the third time?"

Rand picked up the ball and shot it through the hoop. "That makes it four to two. I'll bet you a buck I can tie the game before you make another basket. I'll even give you the advantage." He took three steps backward, placing at least five yards between them, then lobbed her the ball.

"Like candy from a baby." She smirked and set up for her shot. She dipped one shoulder and released, but Rand was remarkably fast on his feet and managed to bat the ball away before it fell into the basket.

He was right there for the rebound and a smooth hook shot evened the score. "It's to you, old girl.

Better brush up on your moves if you want to win your money back."

"My moves don't need any brushing up," she retorted, feeling the familiar exhilaration of the sport rush through her veins. "You were goaltending, Skeeter."

"That's not what a referee would have called it," Rand disputed her accusation. "All I showed was some good defense. Perhaps you're getting a mite slow in your old age, Stilts. I, on the other hand, have reached the peak of my physical prowess."

"And you're going to need it, Skeeter." Julie charged, gearing her body up for action. The next time the ball came sailing across the driveway, she was ready. Suddenly, it was number fifteen, star center for the Granville Golden Bears, who dribbled up the driveway, feinted past her defender and jumped up for two points.

She dodged past him for her own rebound, then cut in front of him for an easy lay-up. "That's what happens to players who get overly confident."

After that comment, the game of one on one began in earnest. It was a no-holds-barred free-for-all. For the first twenty minutes Julie held her own, proud that she was a match for his greater height and strength. After a time, however, Rand started running circles around her. To make matters worse, he kept up an endless stream of taunting chatter designed to break her concentration. She was compelled to dredge up every last vestige of her endurance in order to keep up.

She blocked, she screened, she pivoted and jumped, but Rand anticipated every one of her moves. Her best shots were inside, but because of his height advantage, she was forced to settle for hard-earned field goals. The score showed that her outside shots missed more often than not, forcing her to become reckless.

Julie ran herself ragged, and it wasn't long before she could barely breathe. Finally she had to bow to his greater skill. "You win, Skeeter."

She slumped against the garage door, her breathing strident and labored, her heart thudding heavily within her chest. Her face was mottled from exertion and tendrils of her hair stuck moistly to her skin. She watched in fascination as Rand, with energetic ease she could only envy, jumped high in the air and dunked the ball through the hoop. Kareem Abdul-Jabbar couldn't have done it any better.

"It's over," he decreed shortly, then tossed the ball down the driveway. "But nobody won."

Julie was taken aback by the look on his face, the underlying sadness in his tone. As he walked slowly toward her, she noted that he seemed to be taking no joy in his victory. When he stopped, his stance was deceptively nonchalant, one hand resting on his hip and the other against the garage door.

"I'll get my purse," Julie offered, heaving herself away from the support of the garage, fully intending to make good her debt.

He surprised her by saying, "No, that's not the kind of payment I want."

"What?" Julie frowned her confusion, nonplussed when he swiveled on one heel and imprisoned her body against the garage door.

"This is what I want," he pronounced thickly, taking her chin in his hand.

In the heartbeat before he took her mouth, he gazed deep into her eyes, burning her with a golden brand she'd feel forever. His hands raked through her hair as he claimed her with a hunger that was as elemental as fire. Julie felt as if she had been dormant for months and was just this moment coming alive. She was with Rand, breathed for him, moved for him, lived for him.

She felt every hard plane of his body as she fused herself to him, felt the full extent of his arousal. It had been so long since she'd been in his arms, so long since she'd been able to satisfy her yearning for his taste. She couldn't help herself and reached out for all she craved.

Rand tore his mouth from hers, breathing raggedly. "Julie," he said hoarsely. "Don't do this to me. I'm begging you."

Julie stared back at him, hypnotized by his eyes and too shaken to comprehend his words. With great effort she whispered his name. He came back to claim her mouth with renewed hunger, proclaiming a need as great as her own.

When he roughly pulled himself away, she was stunned. His face was twisted in anger, his breathing uneven and labored, in his eyes was an accusation. "Damn you," he swore through his teeth. "I can never win with you, can I?"

"What are you saying?" she cried out. Tears shimmered on her lashes. Her mouth trembled to keep a sob from escaping. "Why, Rand? Why are you hurting me like this?"

At first it didn't appear he was going to answer her. His body went still. He stared down at her swollen lips and took a long tortured breath. A second later he looked away.

Rand cursed himself for still wanting her so badly, loving her so much. Would he never be free of this torment? Free of wanting what he could never have? He had promised himself that when he saw her again, he would be in control of himself, but all it had taken was one glimpse of her face and the helpless rage he'd been dealing with for seven months had washed over him in waves.

It was time for a little honesty between them. He knew he could still have her in his bed, her response to his kiss told him that. But he had to tell her why he couldn't afford to give in to that temptation. If he acted out his desire, he'd leave part of himself behind each time he had to go away from her.

"I swore when I left you this time, it wouldn't be with my tail tucked between my legs. For years I've lived with the knowledge that you thought you were better than me, and for a long time you were. I put you on a pedestal and you stayed there until Hawaii."

Julie looked up when she heard the agonized strain in his voice. "I don't understand."

"You never did." Rand's accusation cut through her like a knife. "I was fool enough to wear my heart on my sleeve, and you ripped it off. You put me through hell that last day and I've been suffering ever since."

"We made beautiful love that night," Julie reminded him brokenly.

"No. I made love, you were just trying to assuage my thwarted ego."

"How can you say that?"

"Because I know that the only title you want joined with your name is Ph.D. You made it very clear that nobody was to get in the way of your career. Not a lover or a friend and certainly not a husband. Well, I hope that lofty degree of yours keeps you warm on cold nights."

"Husband? You never mentioned marriage."

"I'm not that big a fool. I need a real flesh-and-blood woman, Julie, not some beautiful but heartless goddess who can't admit to mortal weakness. I gave you every chance to come down and join me in the real world, but you refused the invitation.

"Today I needed to prove something to myself so I could forget you and get on with my life, something to keep *me* warm at night. That last night in Hawaii, I felt as if I'd been shot. Today I couldn't resist taking a few potshots at you. I know it was childish, but I needed to retrieve some of the shredded remnants of my pride."

"Your pride!" Julie willed back her tears in the face of such an unfair attack. "You walked out on me," she railed. "I gave my whole being to you that night and the next morning you thanked me for the good time and left."

"That's not what I said," he defended.

"Oh yes you did," she countered fiercely. Her exhaustion fled, replaced by the strength of her anger. "I told you I loved you and you told me goodbye. Goodbye and good luck!"

"The hell I did," Rand bellowed. "I told you I loved you and you said don't stand in the way of my career!"

"Did not!"

"Did too!"

Nose to nose, chin to chin, they glared at each other in mutual frustration. Then, simultaneously, they both realized how ludicrous their behavior was and burst out laughing.

"Will you listen to us?" Rand shook his head in disbelief. "You'd think we were still kids."

Filled with incredible joy, Julie tilted her head and winked at him. "Thank God, we're not." Lifting up on her toes, she pulled his head down and delivered the passionate kiss of a full-grown woman. He was the man she loved and she let him know it.

When she finally moved her lips away, she whispered, "Did you get the message that time?"

"I don't think so," Rand said as he threaded his fingers into her hair. "I'm a little slow on the uptake. You'd better repeat yourself."

"I love you, Skeeter," she murmured against his lips.

"I love you, Stilts," he chanted softly. "So much so, my heart wilts."

"Your poetry is as bad as your singing," she reproved huskily a second before his mouth claimed what was his.

PROPPED UP against the down-filled pillows, Julie reached for another piece of the pastry that had accompanied the pot of hot chocolate they'd ordered. Rand's hand closed over her wrist and the buttery morsel ended up in his mouth. "I need all the sustenance I can get," he excused. "My woman has a voracious appetite and I need to keep my strength up."

Julie wrinkled her nose at him. "And I thought you were at the peak of your physical prowess," she teased lovingly.

"All lies," he confessed. "You've worn me out. I can't keep up with you."

Julie looked out the window of their hotel room and noticed for the first time how many hours had elapsed since they'd left the house. They'd taken a long walk during which they condemned themselves repeatedly for having been so foolish as to let seven months go by without seeing each other. Finally, the sun having set, taking with it the warmth that had taken the edge off the crisp temperature, they'd sought the warmth of the coffee shop at the Buxton Inn.

Ignoring his hot chocolate, devouring her with his wondrous eyes, Rand had reached across the table for her hand and said, "I know a better way to warm up." He'd nodded his head toward the reservations desk in the lobby.

"But we don't have any baggage. They'll know why we're taking a room," Julie had demurred, her body already heated by his suggestion.

"Who cares? I've got everything I need, anyway,' he'd declared and then pulled her up from her chair.

A few moments later, they'd rented a room. The lovely nineteenth-century decor was ignored. Privacy and the high, old-fashioned brass bed were the only things they sought. Wasting few words and even less time, they stripped off their clothes and consummated the declarations they'd made to each other out by the Stites's garage.

The months they'd been apart were forgotten as they'd come together. They'd taken each other with an urgent need that had bordered on starvation. It was a long time before their appetites had been satisfied to the point where other subjects could be introduced.

"There are a few minor details we need to address," Julie stated, willing herself not to be affected by the naked man beside her.

Rand lifted the wicker tray and placed it on the floor beside the bed. His golden-brown eyes drifted slowly over her lush form. From the top of her silvery-blond head to the tips of her toes, he visually inventoried her. "I thought I'd addressed every detail. Is there some part of you I missed?"

"We have to be serious," Julie insisted, fending off his roving hands.

"I am serious." Beneath the sheet, his fingers began moving upward, smoothing the tops of her thighs as he shifted himself closer. He ended up with his head contentedly resting between her full breasts.

Julie was rapidly losing her composure. "We have to work out the logistics of this thing," she cried out in desperation.

Rand lifted his head and stared at her. "Right," he agreed with a mischievous leer. Before Julie could do more than gasp in shock, he grabbed her shoulders and rolled with her. "You can have the top this time and I'll take the bottom," he told her enthusiastically, settling her astride him.

"No, no, no," she wailed.

"Yes, yes, yes," he countered and another hour passed without intelligible conversation.

When Julie recovered, she grabbed for a corner of the sheet and wrapped it mummy-style around herself. She took all the pillows and piled them between them. Ordering him to stay on his own side of the bed, she tried to resume the discussion he'd forestalled earlier.

"Okay, you crazy man, like it or not we're going to talk this time. I want the answers to a few minor questions. For example, where are we going to live?"

"More important, when are you going to make your appearance before the board and earn your new title?" he inquired, resigned to the inevitable settling of mundane details. Julie wanted everything laid out in a neat and tidy package. She wanted the procedures clearly outlined, and although he thought they could play it by ear that wasn't the way his Julie did things.

"Well, since I've completed all the necessary research and passed my orals, I'm fully prepared to accept being Mrs. Randall Maxwell as soon as the paperwork is completed," she informed him, entering easily into his playful analogy. "To be practical, I figure that can all be accomplished by Christmas. What do you think?"

"I had a closer date in mind," Rand replied dryly.

"When?"

"Tomorrow."

After careful consideration, they compromised on the following Monday. Rand had supplied sufficient data to prove that all the necessary documents could be obtained in a couple of days. With a little more negotiation, he'd convinced her that they couldn't afford to wait until Christmas.

The atmosphere became much more sober when they began tackling the problem of their separate careers. Rand suggested that he resign his post at Columbia and apply for a position at USC. Julie as-

tonished him by saying that she was the logical one
to move.

"You have too many people depending on you to
just up and quit," she pointed out. "The institute can
get along just fine without me, but those boys at the
recreation center need you. Your students need you,
Rand. You can't just leave them hanging in the middle of the semester."

"Are you sure you want to give up your position?" he queried, never more serious. If he'd ever
had any doubts about where he stood in her life, she
had just dispelled them. Even so, he wanted to give
her every chance to have exactly what she wanted.
If she gave up her job, he didn't want that decision
to come back and haunt either of them.

"You won't find another position on the East Coast
like you have at Carlton," he cautioned. "One university's basically the same as another for me. I can
teach anywhere. As far as the kids at the rec center
go, there's a new batch all the time. Besides, New
York doesn't have an exclusive on hyper kids. They
can be found anywhere."

Julie was touched by his concern for her future,
but giving up her job at Carlton was something she
felt she really needed to do. With Rand's help she had
taken stock of her life and discovered that she was
ready to do something more with her education than
she had up until now.

She was an expert in her field, loved her subject
and was sure she could convey that enthusiasm in
the classroom. Like the instructor who had inspired
her to take up the study of volcanology, she wanted
to inspire others. "L.A. doesn't have an exclusive on
geophysicists, either. You made a good suggestion a

while back and I've done a lot of thinking about it. Maybe I won't be able to get into research somewhere else, but how about teaching? Do you suppose Columbia could stand another Dr. Maxwell?"

"If you can convince a certain professor that teaching is really what you want to do, he might be able to pull a few strings on your behalf." He leaned over the wall of pillows and ogled her sheet-clad body. "I know he's very impressed by your credentials."

Upon Rand's acceptance of her decision, they talked about buying a big old house in Connecticut. While on that subject, Julie brought up her views concerning a family. Being an only child, she'd longed for brothers and sisters. She hoped to have several children.

Rand's features suddenly tensed. "You remember what I was like as a kid?"

"How could I forget," she tossed back humorously, but he didn't smile in return.

"Odds are that some of our children will be every bit as hyper as I was. It's an inherited thing. His tone conveyed both hope and anxiety. "If we have a bunch of kids, our home might turn out to be a madhouse."

"But they'll have a father who'll understand where they're coming from," Julie returned swiftly, anxious to relieve his worry. "They'll also have a mother who's had plenty of experience dealing with the problem. If you haven't noticed, my darling Skeeter, I've become quite adept at handling you. In fact, I think I'm the very best candidate for the job."

Rand's face lit up in the smile she loved. "Let's make babies." He knocked down the pillow blockade. "If we start right now, we can have our own basketball team by our fifth wedding anniversary or...maybe our fourth...or if we're really efficient, we could have them two at a time...or—"

"Or, we could postpone this discussion until after we're married. I want you all to myself for a while. One-on-one's the only game I'm interested in at the moment. We'll consider team sports later."

She pushed him back to his side of the bed and pointed to the clock. "I think we'd be wise to call our folks," she suggested, her innate practicality taking over once more. "We've been gone for hours, and you know what our mothers are like. By this time, they've probably filed missing persons reports."

"I doubt it," he disagreed. "They're probably making out wedding invitations. But you're right, we should call and let them know the date. Then we can get started on the honeymoon. Suppose we can wedge in a trip back to Hawaii in the near future?"

"Maybe," she responded absently. "It was romantic there, wasn't it?"

"Mmm. And this time if the Sellinghams are around, we wouldn't have to lie to them. We'd really make the most of our time there."

She removed his hand from her breast and reached for the telephone. "You make the most of your time no matter where you are."

"Yeah," he agreed and returned his hand to her breast. "Aren't you glad?" His other hand loosened the snug sheet and skimmed over her body.

"Skeeter!"

"Control yourself, Stilts. You really ought to keep your hands off me long enough to call your folks."

"WELL? WELL?" Will demanded as soon as his wife had·replaced the receiver in its cradle.

"Well what, dear?" Angela countered, a beatific smile on her face. "You shouldn't worry about them. They're adults and perfectly capable of taking care of themselves."

With deceiving casualness she joined her writing partner at the kitchen table. "You were saying, Syl?"

"I think we'd be better off going with beef than ham. Sarah Olson has already promised to make the cake, and I think we can count on Bea Martin for the flowers."

Neither woman acknowledged the man stalking the table. Angela tucked a pencil behind her ear and ran one finger down the lists Sylvia had been making. "That looks like everybody unless you have some suggestions, Will."

"Okay, ladies." Will pulled out a chair, placed his pipe in the ashtray and sat down. "What's going on?"

"I know this will come as a surprise to you, Willard," Angela began breezily, "but Syl and I did know what we were doing. We've always said when it comes to the people you love—butt in."

"Are you talking about Julie and Rand? After this miserable day, how can you think your interference did anything but cause big problems?"

Sylvia and Angela exchanged satisfied smirks. "The darkest moment always comes before the dawn," Sylvia proclaimed. "This miserable day has ended beautifully! Rand and Julie have decided to get married, haven't they, Angela?"

Angela nodded. "In three days."

Will sputtered in disbelief. "Married? Three days? They could've given us a little more time to get used to this."

"We've had twenty-eight years," Angela reminded warmly. "I think that was plenty long enough, don't you Syl?"

"It certainly was," the woman agreed.

Willard rubbed his forehead with his fingertips. "I don't believe any of this."

"I hate to be the type to say I told you so..." his wife's melodic voice trailed off as her husband lifted his head and his face broke into a loving and very satisfied smile.

Harlequin Temptation

COMING NEXT MONTH

#85 LIFETIME AFFAIR Patt Parrish

Ben and Caroline were neighbors battling a
storm together to save his beach house from
destruction. And when the waves subsided, it
was clear that the attraction between them was
as inevitable as the tides. . . .

#86 WITHOUT A HITCH
Marion Smith Collins

She was footloose and freewheeling down the
interstate to a new life in Florida. But one
glance in her rearview mirror and Libby found
herself rerouted. Suddenly, falling in love was
an unavoidable detour!

#87 FIRST THINGS FIRST
Barbara Delinsky

Chelsea's job was to track down missing
children—not runaway executives. But the
moment she found the renegade, hidden away
in a remote Mexican village, she knew what
she'd been searching for . . . all her life.

#88 WINNING HEARTS Gloria Douglas

Six years ago Elizabeth's childish advances
had been spurned by rugged John Logan. Now
a glamorous model, she was ready to take on
the arrogant cattleman. The result was an
electrifying showdown!

TEMP-85-88

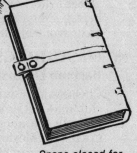

WORLDWIDE LIBRARY IS YOUR TICKET TO ROMANCE, ADVENTURE AND EXCITEMENT

Experience it all in these big, bold Bestsellers— Yours exclusively from WORLDWIDE LIBRARY WHILE QUANTITIES LAST

To receive these Bestsellers, complete the order form, detach and send together with your check or money order (include 75¢ postage and handling), payable to WORLDWIDE LIBRARY, to:

In the U.S.
WORLDWIDE LIBRARY
Box 52040
Phoenix, AZ
85072-2040

In Canada
WORLDWIDE LIBRARY
P.O. Box 2800, 5170 Yonge Street
Postal Station A, Willowdale, Ontario
M2N 6J3

Quant.	Title	Price
_____	**WILD CONCERTO**, Anne Mather	$2.95
_____	**A VIOLATION**, Charlotte Lamb	$3.50
_____	**SECRETS**, Sheila Holland	$3.50
_____	**SWEET MEMORIES**, LaVyrle Spencer	$3.50
_____	**FLORA**, Anne Weale	$3.50
_____	**SUMMER'S AWAKENING**, Anne Weale	$3.50
_____	**FINGER PRINTS**, Barbara Delinsky	$3.50
	DREAMWEAVER,	
_____	Felicia Gallant/Rebecca Flanders	$3.50
_____	**EYE OF THE STORM**, Maura Seger	$3.50
_____	**HIDDEN IN THE FLAME**, Anne Mather	$3.50
_____	**ECHO OF THUNDER**, Maura Seger	$3.95
_____	**DREAM OF DARKNESS**, Jocelyn Haley	$3.95

YOUR ORDER TOTAL	$_____	
New York and Arizona residents add appropriate sales tax	$_____	
Postage and Handling	$____.75	
I enclose	$_____	

NAME _____

ADDRESS _____ APT.# _____

CITY _____

STATE/PROV. _____ ZIP/POSTAL CODE _____

WW3

Take 4 books & a surprise gift FREE

SPECIAL LIMITED-TIME OFFER

Mail to **Harlequin Reader Service**®

In the U.S.
2504 West Southern Ave.
Tempe, AZ 85282

In Canada
P.O. Box 2800, Station "A"
5170 Yonge Street
Willowdale, Ontario M2N 6J3

YES! Please send me 4 free Harlequin Temptation® novels and my free surprise gift. Then send me 4 brand-new novels every month as they come off the presses. Bill me at the low price of $1.99 each — a 13% saving off the retail price. There are no shipping, handling or other hidden costs. There is no minimum number of books I must purchase. I can always return a shipment and cancel at any time. Even if I never buy another book from Harlequin, the 4 free novels and the surprise gift are mine to keep forever.

Name _____ (PLEASE PRINT)

Address _____ Apt. No. _____

City _____ State/Prov. _____ Zip/Postal Code _____

This offer is limited to one order per household and not valid to present subscribers. Price is subject to change.   DOHT–SUB–1

Harlequin Intrigue

Because romance can be quite an adventure.

Available wherever paperbacks are sold or through

Harlequin Reader Service

In the U.S.	In Canada
Box 52040	5170 Yonge Street,
Phoenix, AZ	P.O. Box 2800, Postal Station A
85072-2040	Willowdale, Ontario M2N 6J3

INT-6